FIELDS OF ICE

ARABELLA EDGE studied at Bristol University and left for Australia in 1992. Her first novel, *The Company*, won Best First Book in the 2001 Commonwealth Writer's Prize in the South Pacific region, and was shortlisted for Australia's prestigious Miles Franklin Award 2001. Her second novel, *The Raft*, was published in 2006. She lives with her husband Nick Gaze on the east coast of Tasmania.

ARABELLA EDGE

Fields of Ice

PICADOR

First published 2011 by Picador
an imprint of Pan Macmillan, a division of Macmillan Publishers Limited
Pan Macmillan, 20 New Wharf Road, London N1 9RR
Basingstoke and Oxford
Associated companies throughout the world
www.panmacmillan.com

ISBN 978-0-330-53624-0

1 3 5 7 9 8 6 4 2

A CIP catalogue record for this book is available from
the British Library.

Printed in the UK by CPI Mackays, Chatham ME5 8TD

I wish we could see you in a glass as they do in the fairy tales. Yet how painful it would be to see, yet unable to alter any dreadful difficulty the ships might yet have to overcome.

Jane Franklin to her husband
John Franklin, 1848

For Ann Tait,

My wonderful mother-in-law

Part One

London. May 1848.

I wait, silent, expectant, wary, in the library, the house of Dr Hands, Duke Street, Grosvenor Square by appointment of eight o'clock this evening to see and consult the clairvoyant Ellen Dawson. The maroon velvet curtains with gold trim and tassels have been drawn shut. A silver candelabra stands in the centre of an oval mahogany table, which gleams beneath the dancing wicks. A scent of beeswax mingles with the cloying perfume of an arrangement of arum lilies massed in a Venetian glass vase on the sideboard.

Why are we here? The funereal atmosphere, the stuffiness of this overheated room, a fire burning in the grate despite the mild spring night are surely for theatrical effect? I dare not look my niece in the eye. Seated beside me, Sophy is nervously twisting her handkerchief into tourniquets.

As for Dr Hands, he greeted us with the solicitous

unctuous manner of an undertaker, deferential guide, anticipating wonders, miraculous visions conjured by visiting neophytes yet by the way he tucked his chin into his collar and surveyed the room with professional pride, the scene set and illuminated for his charge, he would not be surprised by them. After all, these spirits are his familiars, part of his repertoire and perhaps my husband, Sir John Franklin, is among them. After a final inspection, a courteous bow, he darts through the half-open door once again leaving Sophy and me alone.

When I glance her way, Sophy manages a smile.

My husband would not approve of such measures. Franklin would abhor these forays into the occult, denounce Dr Hands a treacherous fraud, a veritable brigand, which would bring the colour high to his brow, and a tremor through his right arm. He would march me from this Duke Street establishment and ignore my attempts to placate him by saying there had been no desire to look into futurity but simply to ascertain that which *is now* by means of an extended state of vision.

At this he would throw back his head and laugh, retort that I had an answer for everything whereas he had none, which is the truth – God bless his soul.

I have never met a man so lacking in words so that when he spoke he sounded borrowed, second-hand, reliant on stock phrases. I should have commissioned my good friend Roget to compile a book, a thesaurus of bon mots for every occasion, affectionate billet-doux, epistolary gossip, witty pen portraitures, political dispatches argued with persuasion and cunning. Franklin describes everybody alike as being so amiable and agreeable that I cannot tell one from the other despite my exhortations to seek out the faults and not the virtues only.

There, I allow my thoughts to run as if he were here for me to scold – dear, kind, benevolent husband who would not harm an ant that had ventured across the tablecloth on a lone expedition from the jam dish to the sugar bowl.

Dr Hands now hovers by the doorway. There is a rustle of muslin and lace and a diminutive young woman teeters into the room, perfectly formed like a doll, a froth of golden curls piled high on her head, painted lips accentuated into a cupid bow, a hint of rouge highlighting the cheekbones, and the most striking sapphire-blue eyes which linger unblinking on mine. She cannot be more than a child and I clasp my hands tight, in thrall and with a sense of being duped at the same time.

I would be a fool not to expect trickery, would love to fathom how in the end it is done. Yet I am eager as a child at a pantomime. I long to be astonished, a dangerous state of mind, I know, but I am restless and tired of waiting and listening to people who can tell me nothing of my husband's expedition, indeed do nothing except send one another self-congratulatory missives. I can hear them now, those fine gentlemen striding the assembly rooms of Admiralty House.

From Sir John Barrow, Second Secretary – *former experience has clearly shown that with the resources taken from this country, two winters may be passed in the polar regions – not only in safety, but with comfort;*

The anxiety that prevails regarding Sir John Franklin, and the brave fellows who compose the crews of the two ships, is very natural but somewhat premature; it arises chiefly from nothing having been received from them since fixed in the ice of Baffin Bay, where the last whaling ship of the season of 1845 left them opposite the opening to Lancaster Sound –

and so on.

Now almost three years have slipped by since the *Erebus* and the *Terror* were last seen one month into their voyage tacking close to a berg before they vanished into dense fog and since then no news, not a word.

Despite my pleas and petitions only the *Enterprise* and the *Investigator* commanded by Captain James

Ross and Sir John Richardson have been dispatched north-west in search of my husband's expedition. Instead I must wait for returning whalers whose wild narratives cannot be trusted at all.

Have faith, the polar veterans exhort. No other mission has been so meticulously fitted out, so refined with England's latest inventions. Why, the *Erebus* and the *Terror* are virtually indestructible, have been strengthened to Herculean proportions. Each externally sheathed with copper and stout planking, internally fortified with strong cross and longitudinal beams of Canadian elm, African oak, with iron stanchions and diagonal fastenings. Impervious to ice and independent of wind, I am told, the ships can move at will without sail, powered as they are by steam locomotives, brass twin-bladed retractable propellers engineered by the London & Greenwich Railway. And to reassure me further, they elaborate on the ship's heating systems, tubular boilers pumping steam from wardrooms to cabins.

For the officers' entertainment, a library comprising seventeen thousand volumes including the complete works of Shakespeare, the latest novels from Thackeray and Dickens, geographical magazines and bound copies of *Punch*.

As for the stores, preserved tinned provisions, the

very best purveyed by Goldner's Meat Factory, enough to last five or six years at the most.

No need to worry, my dear, no cause for alarm, the admirals soothe. Relax. Enjoy the winter spas of Evian, Baden-Baden. So Sophy and I trail the continent, anxious, restless, bored.

Your husband has but to find the North-West Passage, they declare. You can count on it, Lady Franklin, *Technology* will take him through. He will be the first to discover a lucrative trade link between the Atlantic and the Pacific. Victory and the ten thousand pound reward will soon be yours, the very name of Sir John Franklin revered throughout the world. Just think of it.

And I do, my Lords, with each passing day. So they cajole and flatter in turns.

Bah! I am sick of the Admiralty, sanctimonious officials, knocking on my door at Spring Street, suggesting that I get out more instead of poring over papers, sifting through every published journal, my husband's instructions, searching for clues.

And the good ladies, simpering behind their fans – why, poor Lady Franklin, I heard Caroline Fox once declaim, spends most days closeted in her room in such an excited state of feeling and has such a sallow look about the skin.

Should get out more – what do they propose – a

tour of the gardens at Kew – when the magnolias are in full bloom. Why, I have ridden at full gallop into Damascus on an Arab stallion leading the charge of a Bedouin tribe brandishing their sabres. Or perhaps a gentle promenade along the gravel paths of the Serpentine?

The *Erebus*. 1847.

September – month of watermelons

I, Canot, who have scullioned at the Coq d'Or, played chef to Mayfair club houses, on good wages and bad Bordeaux, who prided myself on that most difficult simplicity the fillet, now prepare gulls and foxes à la brochette. My wolf waiting to be skinned is a solid hump and a brace of guillemots rigid with frost.

Three stoves and a cooking galley. Four bear-fat lamps smoulder with the consistency of chimneys caught on fire. Damp furs, filthy woollens, cast-off boots, tobacco smoke, the stench of vomit, sick men, hour upon hour, without even a felt curtain to hide me, these make up the reality of my home.

I pace the deck, this endless deck. Uphill work, I wish the ice had given us an even heel, now six feet higher on one quarter than the other. The wind screams over the floes and everything about the vessel is frozen into stalactites. How wretched everything seems. A blank monotony of mural precipices to the north; rough packed hummocks to the east, flatlands to the west stretching mile after mile in smooth sinuous lines like watered silk.

On the darkening plain near the skating ground, the men are carving sculptures; uniformed monkeys hard at a game of billiards, icicles for cues, life-sized chess pieces, skittle alleys; even our Queen Victoria astride a bejewelled elephant, a pack of panthers snapping at her heels. From the crew, bare-breasted mermaids, of course, beseeching Neptune in attitudes of the bordello and desire.

Misshapen gargoyles of the Empire.

This morning, crossing the ice field, a shower of gold and magenta rays flares on the horizon as if fired from a rocket, trailing sparks across the sky. It is impossible to observe the sudden glare of these vivid flashes streaming and shooting fierce as sheet lightning in every direction without fancying accompanying music, the fanfare notes of some celestial choir. Beneath the arched mass of flames, movement and light, I have often stood listening for hours but all I could hear was the halting rasp of my own breath.

The crew shield their eyes from the hypnotic undulations of the Dancing Lights, believe it can undo a man to stare at them for long.

Officer Tutt has wagered a bottle of cognac that he can build St Paul's faster than my Rouen. He staggers a little on his skates, has difficulty shovelling fresh snow.

How my cathedral – those hoary belfries and arched ramparts – soars against poor Tutt's blunt blocks of ice. I am yet to taunt him with an angel, alabaster wings outstretched or a serpent-tongued griffin perhaps, leering from the rooftops, sheer malevolence in talon and claw.

I climb the beginnings of a spiral stairway carved against a turret wall and see from my gothic window which I have yet to fret with fleur de lys that the tackle of the ships, our wooden world, is plumed with perfectly formed crystals like eider feathers. The stalactites of yesterday, jagged and razor-sharp, seem to have evaporated in the infernal mists of frost smoke wreathing the horizon. In this glazed eternity one notices such details.

Nipped, beset, ice-cradled, glued fast on this frozen slab they call King William Land. Shrouded beneath twilight skies, our ship's head points towards a promontory north-eastward but her position changes so constantly there is little use recording it.

*

Each morning Reid the ice-master takes up a knife and notches the tally of our incarceration on the main deck beam.

Seven hundred and twenty-six days on utter darkness borne.

I am suffocating in this place. Need to draw air deep into my lungs once again. There is nowhere to go, this very ship – the rows of hammocks ranged barely an inch apart, the low ceiling on which we bump our heads – we are packed tight as cattle in a pen. And the prospect of another day, squandered, wasted; sand spilling from an hourglass a thousand times over, cloistered in this chilling darkness – an intolerable thought.

Two years since I have been truly alone, complete and at ease with a sense of my own solitude, the innocent pleasure of a country stroll, tangled hedgerows of briar and hawthorn, a skylark's rapturous song.

Not here – miniaturized by vast Arctic plains, oppressed beneath the shadows of the waiting vessels, the men senselessly looping round and around the rink, the constant terror of wolves and bears.

Lately we have forsaken prayer, entombed as we are in this relentless triumvirate – the ice increases. Everything increases, the cold, the fear for the ships. Surely even angels must feel some need for variety.

Officer Tutt kneels on the rough rubble of his

cathedral foundations – no Christopher Wren, he – and unfastens the felt buckles of his skates.

At the peal of the bells, the men trudge back to the ships, each vessel covered in rough canvas.

I follow Tutt's limping progress, skates dangling from one shoulder; driving his wooden stave deep into a fresh bank of snow. A cloud of fog furls around him like the ring around the moon, irradiating for one moment the full spectrum of a rainbow, flaring violet, blue, green, yellow, orange, red, an enchanted sorcerer's cloak only to dissolve colour by colour.

Tutt takes delicate steps up the dirty foot-trodden gangplank, careful not to burn his gloves on icicled ropes tinkling like chandeliers in the wind.

When I wrench open the hatchway – Tutt still too feeble – purple clouds of steam gust from the stovepipes. The very air expelled from our lungs reminds me of a set of duelling pistols fired through dawn mists.

In silence we grope our way down the companionway to the catacombs of the lower decks and the dim soot flicker of lanterns and oil lamps.

When I salute Tutt at the officers' country – sixteen windowless cells barely six feet long and five wide – he pauses, gaunt in his frayed woollen uniform, still sporting threadbare remnants of gold epaulettes.

'Brooks came down while we were dining,' he begins in that well-modulated voice of his which once made him such a favourite with the ladies and the press, 'to say we are driving east like a race-horse and a crack ahead.'

I give a quick deferential nod. 'Very good, sir,' I respond in the brisk, encouraging tone this officer would expect. In the gloom, his face hovers before mine, the texture of whey, that vile milk dish my nurse used to force me to eat as a boy.

Tutt starts at a sound of laughter and the strident chords of a Jewish harp echoing from the great stern cabin.

'Sir,' I venture, 'the officers await you for the evening's theatricals.'

I take my leave before Tutt begins to sob like a child. I am tired of wiping away his tears and explaining they will freeze his lips to his moustache.

Duke Street. Grosvenor Square. May 1848.

The doctor leads his clairvoyant by the hand.

'Ellen will sit here,' he says, motioning a servant to remove the candelabra from the table. Ellen Dawson solemnly takes her place with her back to the curtains. She looks astonishingly young and her coiled hair shimmers in the half-light.

Dr Hands bows and assures us that this is scientific, no mesmerism or fraudulent procedures here. How I wish I could trust him. But I believe in nothing.

At the doctor's instructions, the girl breathes deeply yet keeps her eyes open. Again they rest briefly on mine then settle on a distant point by the door.

'Are you quite comfortable?' asks Dr Hands.

She nods.

'Good,' he whispers. 'You shall go to sleep.'

At the suggestion of drowsiness, drifting, floating, carried downstream on the tides – a tremendous weariness washes over me. I would love to lie still for a moment, sink deeper and deeper into oblivion without a struggle or even a sound.

My head nods. I jerk myself awake – I'm impressionable, I know – and arrange my expression into its usual mask of benign curiosity.

Astonish me, Miss Dawson, I want to say.

'Are you asleep, Ellen?' asks Dr Hands.

She is breathing deeply and evenly.

'Yes,' she says in a low, languid voice.

'Can you hear only me?'

'Yes.'

'Good. Who do you wish to choose as your interlocutor?'

She raises her right arm and points towards Sophy.

My poor niece gasps.

'Miss Cracroft?'

The girl nods.

'Good,' he says again, as if he had always known.

The doctor informs us in a stage whisper that in order to proceed we must avoid loud noises and sudden movements, and each enquiry should be delivered clearly and calmly.

'Please begin,' he intones.

Sophy stares at me frantically.

'Where are the ships commanded by Sir John Franklin?' she finally asks.

The girl begins to shudder. Her satin slippers drum against the parquetry floor. Her fingers grip the arms of her chair.

Theatrical, too tawdry, I think watching her clenched jaws, the whites of her eyes starting to show. I had hoped for something subtler than this amateur performance. Sophy though is transfixed.

We are subjected to more of the same, the neck now rigid, the nostrils distended, that sweet mouth drawn in a rictus grin.

My feet tingle in their tight black patent boots. I shift my weight on the hard leather upholstery. The room is too close by far but perhaps Dr Hands hopes that one of us will swoon and faint.

Suddenly the girl leans forward.

'I have been a long way,' she says. The voice is distant, wavering, but fully alert.

'On the sea and the ice and I saw a ship and several people on it, all gentlemen.'

'Describe them,' exclaims Sophy pressing her palms together as if in prayer.

'One of them was rather old, and rather short and stout, rather dark, with such a nice face.'

She must have seen the daguerreotypes of the

captains and their officers, the series I commissioned before the *Erebus* and the *Terror* set sail, which were published in every newspaper and periodical in the land.

I'm no fool but I am startled by Sophy's enraptured expression.

'Is he quite well, or does he look ill or unhappy?' she asks, sitting bolt upright, a flush in her cheeks.

'He is well and looks happy and comfortable but perhaps—'

The girl falters.

'But he seems rather anxious – yet they have plenty of salt beef and biscuits to eat and they wear fur and smell of brandy.'

I can endure no more.

'Ask which direction the vessels are pointing,' I hiss.

At this the girl's arms begin to flail in the motion of a stricken bird.

'A cloud is there before me,' she cries.

Two sovereigns for this! I want to stamp the floor in exasperation.

Instead, I stifle a yawn and patiently fold my hands on my lap.

'But wait.'

The clairvoyant fixes me with her gaze, the blue eyes quite unseeing.

'I can espy another ship with this one – and two more not very far away and a captain – tall and lean, scanning the horizon through his glass.'

'Why, it must be dear Captain James Ross,' Sophy declares, rising to her feet.

Softly the doctor tiptoes forward and directs my niece to her chair.

'I cannot tell,' Ellen continues in a thin papery voice, 'because the cloud has come down again.'

Poppycock, time to take our leave.

'But wait—'

I've waited long enough, only to subject myself to a retinue of fools – charlatans all, eager for the coins in my purse.

I am old and tired – yet I sit in parlours half lit, Sophy at my side, fossicking for miracles, for someone to tell me my husband is alive. *They wear fur and smell of brandy.*

John doesn't drink, for goodness' sake.

As I nudge Sophy to say enough is enough – the clairvoyant lets out a piercing shriek, which makes my niece jump clean out of her skin.

'The nice old gentleman is clear to me now,' Ellen cries. 'And his cabin is endowed with two portraits of ladies.'

'Of course,' Sophy exclaims, close to tears. 'The Queen and my aunt. Do you see the other lady?'

Ellen Dawson sighs and shakes her head.

Then her words tumble in a rush.

'You must tell her all I have told you – but if she heard me telling it, it would upset her – poor thing—'

Poor thing, I who have scaled the highest mountain peaks in New Zealand and Tasmania.

But still the girl continues in a strange affecting staccato, 'You stop with her – you are always with her now – you must do all you can to comfort and soothe her – and all will be right.'

Sophy sobs into her handkerchief.

I am touched by my niece's affection, that unswerving loyalty to her aunt, which gives me all my strength and sometimes frightens me a little. She will never marry and in some imperceptible way, with no deliberate influence on my part, I wonder if I am responsible for her fate, Sophy the spinster, shadows of grey streaking her temples, hair scraped back from that pencil-sharp parting. And I the sole recipient of her unbridled love – not quite healthy, perhaps.

'Make your mind easy,' the girl continues, 'for all is well, all is quite right.'

The doctor folds his arms and gazes around with a self-satisfied smile. The spectacle must be over and

I have learned nothing from the two gold sovereigns pressed in his palm. Complete hum. Once again I will leave these sessions with swollen feet and the telltale thump of a migraine behind my eyes.

'Is that all, Ellen?' he asks.

Instead of gratifying him with a demure nod of the head, the girl stares straight at me instead.

'There is a man standing behind the lady,' she announces, 'he is placing his hands on the lady's head, his fingers are slender and searching. Hope is large, he says.

'That's good, that's a good thing for you – that will be of use to you.'

At her words I start for I've told no one about my visit to Dr Deville, the renowned phrenologist at the Royal Institution lectures.

I begin to feel uncomfortable beneath the girl's gaze, that stark expressionless face.

There is something wheedling about her tone, which captures the essence of Deville's voice as if he were here, massaging my scalp, leaning forward breathless with observations – *is not combativeness large, yes, and that's a good thing for you. Ideality is large, and you feel poetry very strongly and when you write letters you show it in your expressions – you are seldom at a loss for words.*

How does this girl know unless they are in cahoots together, but surely not Deville, a respected member of the Royal Society?

Ellen has lowered her eyes, picture of parlour-room decorum.

I confess I am quite shaken.

Dr Hands brings the clairvoyant round, soaring upwards, up, up and out from the depths, out of her slumber. At the snap of his fingers, her face is stilled and smooth. Deville has gone. And my husband, the kind old gentleman, what has he become?

Sophy and I walk home in silence, for I am careful not to betray my emotions. Yes, I am astonished.

I had written a personal account of my encounter with Deville in my diaries, dusty volumes now stacked at the bottom of a trunk, weighed with Pompeian mosaic, Egyptian mummy jars, stuffed lizards, two plaster busts of Tasmanian Aborigines, still wrapped in brown paper.

Unpacked, unread, twenty years back. I had even forgotten the promising prognosis of those youthful entries – *hope is large – that's good – that will be of use to you.* And indeed my heart had brimmed large for love, marriage to a man I dared not name, Peter Mark Roget, not even in code. Fool that I was.

Sophy looks frail, careworn tonight. I kiss her on the forehead before she retreats along the hallway and I seek solace in the Japan Room upstairs.

Kicking off my boots, I hobble towards the divan, so richly cushioned and brocaded, such genius in the extravagant beaten-copper shelves, the porcelain vases from Nagasaki, the ebony lacquer cups, silks framed in gilt mouldings – an elaborate eight-panelled screen of cherry blossom set beside the window. I unbutton the mother-of-pearl fastened high at the collar of my gown, slip out of layers of taffeta and lace, struggle with the insufferable hooks, the endless bows and ribbons.

It would cheer me to wear my Japanese grenadine clasped with silver and gold, but I don't have the strength. Instead I reach for the comfort of my old cashmere shawl. Besides there is no one to see me, except Ellen Dawson perhaps rolling the whites of her eyes, omniscient, stern as a sibyl, deciphering meaning in feverish ink scrawls – so many journals, I blush to think of such industry, one entire volume devoted to a three-week visit to Leamington Spa with a second cousin I no longer recall.

Yet how could this Ellen Dawson begin to apprehend the whispered gossip of twenty years past?

I plump the bolster, and stretch out on the divan,

such a relief to rest one's creaking bones – at fifty-six no longer young. How have I aged so?

I should not attend let alone pay for these experiments in extended vision – and if word got out I would be dismissed as foolish, hysterical, a muddle-headed female who sets up for a prophet despite the fact that I am fairly sceptical myself.

But I only have to open my ears to the dreams and visions, the clamour of voices from girls and women all over the country, those psychic sightings of my husband either printed in the newspapers or arriving daily in my postbag.

I confess to a fondness towards a Mrs E of Bolton, for whom no detail goes unnoticed – observing in her correspondence the exact time difference between her home town and the Canadian Arctic – *when the hour there was nine or ten am (four or five pm at Bolton)* she would say. Sadly however her travels over the seas, the jagged maze of the ice, the pious tableaux she conjured – *Sir J. was reading prayers to the crew who knelt in a circle, with their faces upwards, looking to him and appearing sorrowful* – signify nothing.

And the resounding chorus of illiterates, seamstresses, scullery maids, perfectly uninstructed, unable to read or write, who being cast in a mesmeric state are capable of placing their finger on a map showing the exact position of the stricken ships on the north-west side of Hudson's Bay. And the lunatic siren songs from the insane – *My lady, I have took the liberty of thus a-Dressing you with a Line through whose hands I hope will forward to you this remarkable dream which I often found too true . . . I saw in my dream 2 air Bloons a great distance off rising just like the moon – I said in my dream to myself There's Sir J. Frankland.*

No help at all. Yet I am drawn to dear Captain Coppin, the Aberdeen surveyor from the Board of Trade who only last month wrote pressing me to check the truth of his four-year-old daughter, Louisa, or Weesy as she was called among her siblings. Having died eight months past from gastric fever she first appeared distinctly to the three older children proclaiming that the banker next door had expired, which on examination proved to be the case.

I am intrigued by Coppin, bluff, no-nonsense whaler, paterfamilias of a household of grieving women – Weesy constantly showing them scenes which he could not describe. He confessed to having penned an earlier missive but had hidden it instead in a desk drawer, quite alarmed and ashamed by how I might interpret the events that had taken place behind his respectable locked doors.

After subsequent visitations from Weesy, Ann the

eldest daughter quite by chance posed the question: *Is Sir J. Franklin Alive?*

In answer, according to Captain Coppin, the windows flew open wide, the nursery filled with ice and a blue flare floated back and forth across the dim corners of the ceiling. You could see the children's hoary breaths in the chilled room. Above the cot beds, a ship shone brightly embayed in a narrow creek between two mountains of snow, and another glimmered from a distance. When Ann, shivering and entranced, asked which part of the Arctic Ocean, the vessels were situated, the scene vanished and round-hand letters unfurled in grey smoking patterns, *Erebus and Terror, Sir John Franklin, Lancaster Sound, Prince Regent's Inlet, Point Victory, Victory Channel.*

I would impress on your Ladyship the necessity of giving such orders to the Commanders of the last Expeditions going out as would cause a diligent search in Prince Regent's Inlet and into the vicinity of Cape Walker as I am certain that Sir J. Franklin is there and nowhere else in the Arctic as predicted by this Child, Captain Coppin concluded in an excited tone.

Studying the letter – *the vicinity of Cape Walker* – I recalled a conversation with my husband three months before he was due to set sail. He was gazing deep in thought into the fire, with the same brooding downcast expression that had afflicted him ever since he received news of the command, when he turned to me and said: 'Jane, recollect if I find any difficulty, I shall seek to return by the American continent, and if I fail in that I shall go up by the Great Fish River and so get to the Hudson Bay territory.'

The exact route which last year Dr Richard King had first put forward, declaring he would lead the rescue mission himself.

And I would not listen.

Exhausted as I am, I creep from the divan to the escritoire and riffle through my papers – pleas to our Queen, the American President, financiers, philanthropists, press barons, friends. No one left off the list – even Captain Coppin, who has agreed to subsidize the next Arctic venture in the supply ship, the *Albert*.

At last I find Dr King's scrawl scratched on cheap paper dated June 10th 1847 – begging permission to navigate the Great Fish River as he had accomplished ten years earlier and guide the men of the *Erebus* and *Terror* – which they had probably been forced to abandon – to depots of food.

Of course I rejected the advice of Dr King, who had scorned, nay ridiculed my husband, spreading rumours that Franklin would form the nucleus to an iceberg if he were chosen, that his expedition would become a lasting blot in the annals of our voyages of discovery, who proceeded to slander Captains Ross and Richardson intimating they had no intention to search for the lost vessels but desired to achieve the Passage instead, who decreed large-scale sea-rescue missions doomed to failure and so on until, provoked beyond measure, the Arctic Council ruled out King's preposterous proposal.

And I had been instrumental in that final decision.

Of Dr King, himself, I wish to say nothing – I declared before a meeting of esteemed polar captains. *I do not desire that he should be the person employed.*

The problem with appointing Franklin to lead the expedition, certain Admiralty members concurred – oh I can hear the whispering of the scoundrels still, Sabine, Back, Dr King among them – lay in the fact that at fifty-eight, he was simply too old, grown corpulent, somewhat rusticated after seven years' desk work as Governor of Van Diemen's Land, and since his unfortunate dismissal from that place had become desperate to restore his reputation. A desperate man is a dangerous commander. Why not send the forty-four-year-old Captain Ross instead?

The jockeying for this contest – discoverer of the elusive North-West Passage – required an intense behind-the-scenes rivalry, a fierce competition involving family connections, the secret influence of powerful allies. And who better equipped to excel at such a task than I? Suffice to say, the timing of our return from that ungrateful isle could not have been more propitious. The vile penitentiary had trained me well.

Eagerly I redoubled my efforts, lobbied tirelessly on my husband's behalf, insisted he would die of disappointment if he were refused command. Ceaselessly I wrote to every interest, petitioning the presidents of the Royal and Geographical Societies, the Lord Commissioners, the Arctic Council. Even the Second Secretary, Sir John Barrow himself, who would shrink from my gaze whenever I strode the marble corridors of Admiralty House.

I succeeded in my campaign because only I with my politician's eye unveiled a central problem – first choice Sir William Parry had declined, the second, Captain Ross, refused point blank – and only in me had these polar explorers confided they were married, they were in love, had achieved the pinnacle of their careers – were half sick of shadows, the constant voyages to the ice.

Third choice, that silly pup James Fitzjames fresh from China, rejected on account of inexperience and youth.

Soon opinion swayed, as I knew it would, in favour of Franklin. Besides, he carried all the right credentials

– English, Anglican, Companion of the Royal Guelphic Order, a gentleman – in short a national guarantee as the newspapers would declaim.

Yet having denounced Dr King, experienced explorer, I now seek meaning in the ghostly apparitions of this Weesy, a deceased four-year-old child. I must be mad.

I glance at the daguerreotype plate of my husband I always keep on my side table. It was taken on the very day he set sail. Sometimes inspecting my husband's stern face, the dark shadows beneath his eyes, the dejected down-turned mouth, the brass buttons of his uniform pulled tight across his chest, I wonder if Franklin's adversaries might have been right.

Ah, Franklin, I miss your shy gallant manner, your baffling formality, that good-natured boyish smile. I have never before met such sincerity in a man.

I still have your letter from Paris where you waited to take command of the *Rainbow* bound for the Mediterranean station – *I am writing to you now after my friends have retired to bed in the hope of this reaching you on the anniversary of our wedding – my constant thoughts and most affectionate wishes will be with you. May we both fervently thank the Almighty to render each other and those around us happy.*

I smiled when I read your note, so polite and

reserved. I imagined you seated alone in some hotel parlour scowling into the dim empty darkness. You wanted to compose a sonnet, a love poem. Instead, you set each sentence plain and clear like a true captain's standing orders, lest they run from your pen and contort your thoughts into the most devilish of mariner's knots.

I replied more fully, confessed that all my personal vanities and sensibilities had been absorbed in you and I felt no satisfaction in any sense of superiority, such as you sometimes attributed to your wife, but the greatest joy and purest delight in all that you possessed over me.

I rest my head on the pillows. I must sleep. Will sleep. But endlessly my mind runs helter-skelter – Dr King had been the first to propose a search mission. And because professionally and personally I disliked him, I pulled every string to have him discredited. Now three crucial years have elapsed while Sophy and I drifted across the continent lulled by the Admiralty dispatches – no news, no cause for alarm.

If only I had given Dr King the support he deserved he might have returned victorious where others will not, but here I speak as a politician whereas I am a mere woman who should fret and wait, pacing a widow's walk, scanning the empty seas like a whaler's wife.

Should, *if*, desolate harbingers of the past, the future unknown.

Nagging us with uncertainties, chivvying us along paths we knew we should have taken, *if*, *if*, quarrelsome, tireless, constant as a metronome.

Again, I glance at my husband's daguerreotype, yellowing and fast-fading.

Even now when I dust the glass the reflection gleams back at me. The expression defeated, recriminating. What did you hope to achieve, it says, and what have I become?

I slide open the secret panel to my escritoire, reach for a phial of laudanum and inhale the pungent scent. A few drops won't harm.

The *Erebus*. 1847.

October – month of pomegranates and figs

Osmer the purser used to fuss around the stores like a broody hen, notebook in hand, ticking off each item, stalking the bread room fitted with bins holding rice, oatmeal and flour; the spirit room, inner sanctum of Madeira and claret, the sailors' grog tubs of rum, the officers' fine French vintages, brandy, champagnes and cognacs, Sir John Franklin's fragrant boxes of Havana cigars.

Yet nothing delighted the purser more than surveying Goldner's patented meat preserves ranged shelf after shelf against thick mortar walls. Adjusting his pince nez, he would study each label and eagerly lick the tip of his pencil before intoning in a nasal drawl – *fourteen preparations of veal, thirteen kinds of beef, seven types of mutton and four varieties of lamb* – and dutifully I would follow, unable at times to stifle a yawn.

Still he compiled his interminable lists: canned capons, turkeys, geese, ducks, pigeons – a selection of game including guinea fowl, venison, jugged hare, partridge, pheasant, ptarmigan, grouse – the latter curried or in onion sauce. At this he would dart me an enraptured smile – *Quite remarkable, wouldn't you say, Canot?*

The purser inventoried whole lobsters in the shell, stewed eel, salmon steaks, real West Indian turtle, Yarmouth bloaters, mackerel lightly salted and smoked.

As for the premium line of *French Dishes*, his pencil fairly flew across the page: beef à la Flamande, calf's tongue piquant, truffled pheasant breast and teal en salmi, not forgetting the condiments – prawn, oyster, mushroom and shrimp.

Good-humoured, amiable Osmer, whose pleasures lay in a pinch of snuff after dinner and thrashing the officers at chess, now keeps to his quarters intent on obsessive games of patience with himself. Sometimes in the rare intervals when the winds have ceased, I can hear a rapid slap of cards against the table, the bird wing flutter as each deck is cut and spliced, expert as a croupier's in his practised hands.

Now I am in charge of his ledger book, the inventories, noting the barrels of salt beef, herring, pemmican – the French lines long gone – the last remaining tins – two hundred and five in all – whenever I venture into those empty echoing chambers where my assistant Coffin has taken to hiding, curled on a pile of rags night after night.

I nudge open the door to the bread room and call out his name softly as if luring a stray cat. But all I can hear is the swift scuttle of vermin. How Coffin thinks he can sleep here, God only knows, giggling and whispering to himself in the dark.

I hurry past the wardroom until I reach the galley where enshrined in His Great Berthing Deck my God awaits me – Frazer's Patent Stove – monstrous Beelzebub hissing steam and blue flames. Six fiendish burners smoulder in the oven and the greatest torment devised in Satan's principality, a hand-powered pump, blistering my palms raw each time I draw water from iron tanks fastened in the lower decks.

The library my night refuge, narrow, mildewed, mahogany hall, coldest part of the ship. Two thousand volumes glazed with ice.

Yesterday, with much sorrow, finished *The Vicar of Wakefield* for the sixth time. Curled in this dripping den, I pull my cloak closer, curse the guttering lamp and reach for Mary Shelley's *Frankenstein*. I have arrived at the Moderns too soon. Each page sears through my gloves like a knife. Again those damned puppy whines, an incessant roar of bees.

I am surrounded by mountains of ice which admit of no escape and threaten every moment to crush my vessel. The brave fellows whom I have persuaded to be my companions look toward me for aid but I have none to bestow. The cold is excessive and many of my unfortunate comrades have already found a grave amidst this scene of desolation.

At dawn I toss the book aside for I know how it will end. Strange to think that our polar predicaments have spawned a literary genre of sorts among good ladies of intellect and taste.

A gale will spring from the west, the ice pushed northward will crack and soon the passage south will open perfectly free wide as the Thames.

Frankenstein dies, and the monster, of course, poor creature lost on ghostly plains. Walton's crew rejoice for soon they will return.

England – I no longer believe in such a place.

Yet I, Canot, was once a man of comfort who liked to take his ease in a deep leather chair by an apple-wood fire, a glass of muscatel within reach and perhaps a volume of Parry's *Narrative to the North Pole* balanced on his knees.

Oh, Parry – what admirable simplicity and real superiority were apparent in those unpretending phrases. How simply he stated: 'We were dying of hunger', and what images of grandeur those simple words called up giving us the facts in every line.

How can a man's life take such an unexpected turn?

Caught unawares, seduced by power to be sure.

At the beginning, you could say I was flattered.

I had become something of a favourite among members of the Admiralty in the Grosvenor Club where for captains and officers I cooked a stolid repertoire of roast beef and Yorkshire pudding, eel pies, grilled turbot – and how they roared for my suet dumplings.

Nothing fancy or refined for the British navy, not for these Lincolnshire lads salmon in aspic or feather-light soufflés, spun sugars and caramels for which I am renowned.

The night before the *Erebus* and *Terror* were due to sail on their mission north, all the noted names of the Admiralty had gathered in the well-proportioned Banquet Hall for the grand finale in a week of flags, bunting, penny whistles and impassioned patriotism penned by the press.

Strange for I had woken that morning with a mild fever, an unexpected premonition of dread. A thin dawn light filtered through my attic window and I considered dispatching the maid – sweet Jeanette, who had tiptoed from my bed at midnight with kisses and caresses and promises of eternal love – to send word that I was indisposed. Yet ever the professional, I roused myself from a fitful doze. Some may call me vain, fastidious even, but I have always taken care with my toilette. Relished the morning ritual, perfumed soap, the warm lathered caress of pure badger bristle – no expense spared in the shaving brush ordered from Jermyn Street – the rasp of a sharpened blade against my jaw. I trimmed the points of a fashionably thin French moustache and parted my hair on one side, just so, to hide the receding widow peaks of my brow.

My eyes, my best feature, almond-shaped, thick-lashed, the irises flecked green and gold, stared back appraising my efforts in the glass. At thirty, not bad, Monsieur Canot.

Ready once again for work, I dressed for the event as usual in freshly pressed livery.

It would be an understatement to say that the Grosvenor Club Banquet Hall has always exuded an atmosphere of serious purpose. And how could it not with its ornate high ceiling decorated in rose emblems of white and gilt, the Venetian marble fireplace carrying the arms of Charles II, the silver hands of the grandfather clock charting thirty-two points of the compass across a map of Europe from the Spanish north coast to the Baltic.

And that day was no exception. The officers resplendent in full-dress uniforms were already deep in conversation when I approached with the claret.

Stately, silver-haired Second Secretary Sir John Barrow at the head, flanked by Sir John Franklin and his commanders James Fitzjames and Francis Crozier, and their newly appointed lieutenants, fine-looking gentlemen, graced with charming ready smiles.

As head chef and expert sommelier, I prided myself as a true master of deference and decorum, which was why the Admiralty requested I attend as butler on these occasions, gliding silently across the parquetry floor, serving course after course as if they were guests at some enchanted feast, the dishes all laid out for pleasure, the crystal flutes filled by some invisible presence.

Privy to secret government information that would cost my life to disclose, I had won a reputation as too much a professional of the old school ever to utter a single word. Always best not to decipher the debates and discussions – the manning of ships, the massing of troops, voices reverberating through the hall like the steady beat of drums from some distant battlefield.

Decanter in one hand, I gently made my way from shoulder to shoulder.

Sir John Barrow was riffling through a pile of documents from a box beside him. He unfolded a letter and shook his head.

'This man directly petitioned us,' he announced. 'Wrote that three nights following, a person appeared to him in a dream and said, "Go with Captain Franklin and he will be crowned with success." '

At this, Franklin flushed and sneezed into his handkerchief. He was suffering from a bad bout of influenza and I congratulated myself on the first course, a restorative French onion soup. I had been instructed to place a jug of water on the table beside him – he was a teetotal, God-fearing soul.

Adjusting his lorgnette, Sir John peered again at the missive and read out loud.

'And not having the smallest thoughts of such things before, and hearing of dreams having led to great discoveries, I put some confidence in this and make bold to offer my services should a steward of my description be wanted.'

Sir John paused and shot Fitzjames an enquiring glance.

'Well, sir,' he said. 'I find no record of this Richard Wall.'

Never could there be a more amiable figure than

Franklin's first in command with his alert animated face, those brown eyes full of good humour and meaning.

'He was sent word of engagement,' Fitzjames replied, 'and this man Wall pledged he would be in London by Friday. Except—'

The officer fished an envelope from his pocket. 'I was very much surprised to receive this,' he said, 'from Wall's wife, sir.'

I happened to be at Fitzjames' side and a faint scent of lavender wafted from the paper in his hand.

'This lady is most indignant to discover that her husband has made an engagement to join our expedition, through a dream and without consulting her, sir.'

A murmur of disbelief ran among the men. Fitzjames darted Sir John an appealing smile and cleared his throat.

'I must beg to tell you, sir, that he shall not go,' he began, '– I will not let him have his clothes. He must be mad ever to think of leaving a comfortable home, to be frozen in with the ice, or torn to pieces with bears; therefore I am determined he shall not leave Gosport, so I hope you will not expect him. Yours, sir etc. and so forth, Mary W.'

The Second Secretary looked at the paper with distaste.

Franklin mopped his brow and gazed feverishly, benignly on as if this exchange did not affect him in the least. Seated opposite, Crozier gave a snort of laughter and drained his glass, which I refilled.

'I could have manned both ships with every captain in the land,' Barrow declared. 'Yet this woman dares deny us a steward and a good one at that. I understand this Richard Wall served under Nelson in the *Victory*. Am I not right?'

By now, I was now concentrating on serving the soup, a highly refined skill I am sure few recognize.

With a resigned air, Fitzjames slid the missive towards the Second Secretary who filed it away and snapped the box shut.

During the toasts to the north, I hurried across the room and slipped behind the servants' green-baize partition. In the kitchen, I found everything in order. Ready with the trolley, I swung open the double doors.

The roast beef proved an incomparable success, parsnips, sprouts done a treat although at times such as this, I yearned for the impetuous fizz and glamour of Parisian cuisine.

When I reached Sir John, I found him scrutinizing me as if I were one of his elite corps recruits.

'No wife, Canot, no family ties?' he enquired. 'No one to hinder your actions or get in the way.'

'No, sir,' I replied relishing his pleasure in the fragrant burst of steam rising from the bain marie.

'Quite alone then, Canot?'

'Count me a free spirit, sir. No binds hold me here.'

There I had said it. Trapped.

Sir John and his officers glanced at one another in secret communication.

'My good fellow, we have a proposition to make,' Sir John finally announced. 'What do you say to an appointment as chief steward in Her Majesty's ships?'

Franklin gave me the briefest of smiles.

'Capital, Canot,' he said and sneezed once again. I noticed he had barely touched the food on his plate.

'You are privileged indeed to be joining our expedition.'

No home and hearth in Gosport, no children to dandle on my knee, no fierce, loving wife to fire letters to the Second Secretary of the Admiralty, pioneer of the British Empire and already a favourite with our young Queen.

Somehow I managed to station the trolley by the sideboard where I waited to serve the port.

It is one thing, I wanted to say, to marvel at heroic deeds, explorers braving Arctic snow and desert sands – remarkable to hear that young Chivers taught himself to write with his left hand seeing that his right arm had been hacked off by savages on a reconnoitre to Damascus – but quite another to actually volunteer and join them.

'I propose a toast, Canot,' one of the young officers called, 'to the finest chef in Mayfair.'

Once the cheering and the pounding of fists against the table had quietened, I returned with a curt bow to the kitchen. Word had spread fast around the club.

Canot had been handpicked, recruited as chief steward on the Franklin expedition to the North-West Passage.

Later congratulated by all from the proprietor already ordering champagne for a group of journalists huddled in the hallway to the pretty chambermaids on whose blushes and flirtatious smiles I should have preyed – *I beg to tell you, sir, he shall not go. He must be mad ever to think of leaving a comfortable home, to be frozen in with the ice, or torn to pieces with bears* – I was escorted to the door.

'Been a pleasure, best of luck, Canot,' the proprietor said shaking my hand. And I found myself on the marble steps of the Grosvenor Club alone.

I trudged the rain-soaked streets to my quarters, a pleasant Soho attic room to pack my bags, or kit, so I am told.

That night I tapped on Jeanette's door. Not a sound

or a shaft of light beneath the threshold. I imagined her with another beau and the hallway felt silent and cold.

Ah, for mistresses, mothers. And wives. *I must beg to tell you, sir, he shall not go – I will not let him have his clothes.*

No Second Secretary, captain or courtly officer to greet me as I climbed the gangplank. Instead, a dirty looking child dressed in a loose pair of pantaloons belted around the hips led me in the dignified capacity of midshipman's boy across wet slippery decks. My ears rang with the shrill whistles and calls of the boatswain and his mates rousing a helter-skelter of footsteps to the tune of 'haul, hoist, let go, belay, turn up, d'ye hear there?'

The *Erebus*'s master scanned the frantic activity as a cat's cradle of pulleys and chains lowered the stowage – at one port coals heaved on board, at another wood and provisions – calling out that a ship down by the bows was harder to handle whereas a ship down by the stern would be slower. What world was I in, I asked myself, careful not to trip over ropes coiled on their cleats, the youth sprinting sure-footedly ahead. A Babel of tongues clamouring to keep 'the hawse clear while the ship was at anchor and see that she was not girt with her cables'.

There were bands and speeches, endless parades, prayers of course, interminable divine services, for Sir John Franklin was a pious man, intoning gruffly from his gilt-edged Bible.

Then the deck lurched beneath my feet and the *Erebus* began to lumber through the silted estuary towards a glint of open waters.

I watched the mudflats recede and the faithful crowds retreat to toast our triumphant departure with gin and ale. Gulls swung above our wake in lazy rhythms. I thought of Jeanette nestled against me as we slept. I even mourned my childhood home perched on precipitous cliffs outside the granite ramparts of Saint Malo; the ruined lookout tower where, as a boy, I would thrill at the rush of evening tides, such a cold savage sea, threshing bronze garlands of kelp.

Here I sit, shivering, chilled to the marrow of my bones in the ruins of this library, chintz curtains laced with rust; oak beams warped and bulged against the bulwarks. Crammed with memoirs, sonnets, novels, manifestos, the swollen shelves creak beneath their load. An occasional burst of glass from some cabinet scatters broken shards across a rug once brightly patterned with unicorns and other heraldic beasts.

A constant rustle from one cobwebbed corner – rats, which I should hunt, had I the cunning and strength.

Bedford Square. May 1848.

The candle gutters in its wick, the tallow worn to a nub. I wake to the sound of gulls massing and mewling following the bloodied wake of dab catchers racing the ebb tides to Billingsgate. Such urgency in those frantic cries.

I listen for the thrush in the mulberry outside to let out one long trilling note, which will be echoed by another and another until the sycamores in the square beyond resound with their song.

Dawn chorus, mournful, elegiac, no longer joyous, rousing me to a new day as it once did when I was a girl.

Shouts in the hallway, I sit bolt upright, hardly daring to breathe, news at last. Captain Ross in the *Investigator* has discovered the ships, the crews alive, and my husband making light of the ordeal, tightening a notch on his belt – see how I've lost my paunch.

Footsteps up the stairs two at a time. I smooth my hair, reach for my shawl.

The door flies open.

'Mama.'

My stepdaughter.

I lie back and draw the sheets to my chin. Eleanor marches towards the divan. She stands over me, tall, imperial, her hat askew, ringlets undone, black eyes flashing, just like her mother, Anne Porden, the lamented and renowned bluestocking poet.

By the determined set of Eleanor's jaw, the tilt of her chin, the pout of that full-lipped mouth, I know what she wants. How dare she intrude so early unannounced like this?

'John and I intend to be married—' she begins.

I turn my face to the wall. Reverend John Philip Gell, fawning pious pastor who stuck to us fast like a leech in Hobart Town, currying sinecures, favours, courting my husband's daughter who ran wild as a gypsy. I have always done my best by the girl, patiently coaxing her catechism, her letters, drawing lessons, musical recitals only to be disappointed. She'd write to her father in so bad a hand that I was obliged to suppress the missive, despite the inevitable tears and tantrums.

I have long harboured a cherished desire that Eleanor might marry one of my sister Mary's boys for Gell has never shown anything beyond a disposition to amuse himself. But I resigned myself to Gell as a good second best. For one who is not over-fastidious in small matters, I had hoped he might exert the most useful influence over Eleanor's character, but in this I have been proved wrong.

Gell watches my purse strings like a lynx. With all my public appeals, I must meet every conceivable expense, fund new subscriptions, endless dispatches, not to mention travelling allowances for my benefactors request personal appointments. Soon I hope to meet the gin distillery tycoon Felix Booth in New York and need to be suitably attired for the occasion.

How many times do I have to explain that if it makes the difference between life and death, spend I will, not only my own private assets but the generosity of others keen to find my husband alive and well, restored as rightful hero to the people of England.

Yet still Eleanor persists, see how she brandishes a sheaf of documents clenched in one hand.

I close my eyes.

Her voice high pitched, grating as she storms and rants, she is twenty-four and in love, wants to get married and needs something to live on.

Want, *need* – these are the words you would read if you sliced her through, like a stick of Brighton rock.

'My father,' she exclaims, 'fully expected to return.

Had he done so he would eagerly have made a provision for his only daughter about to be betrothed.'

To a certain extent this is true – on his demise Eleanor would inherit the considerable estate Franklin received from his first wife. This stepdaughter of mine is aware she could be a wealthy woman and the clergyman she insists on marrying comfortably set up for life.

Except – her father is not yet dead. And I have been given power of attorney to use his income as I think fit. Believe me, I have pored over the calculations, added and subtracted the sums, and should the *Enterprise* and the *Investigator* fail, I've the resources to finance five more ships at the very least, stage the most comprehensive rescue operation ever witnessed on these shores. I have even put forward a two thousand pound reward. Surely she should be grateful for that.

Instead Eleanor complains all the time that I am squandering her inheritance. Would prefer to walk up the aisle in a fine gold-threaded gossamer gown than see her own dear sweet Papa again.

I stare into those furious eyes of hers.

'I am prepared,' I declare in a soothing tone, 'to make a generous allowance of three hundred pounds.'

Eleanor's face crumples. 'Three hundred pounds,' she exclaims, 'barely enough for us to maintain an appearance.'

'You must understand,' I say, 'that money will never be so precious to me as it is at this time. You will have to wait.'

She bites her lip, not prepared to admit defeat.

We have waged war before and become quite adept in selecting the weaponry at our disposal. But of late, Eleanor is becoming dull and predictable, easy to checkmate, making false moves with her king and queen, *my* father, *my* mother – relying on Gell and his coterie of friends, weak flanks of bishops, knights, rooks.

She gazes at me imploringly.

'Surely,' she begins, 'if Papa has undergone great suffering, it must be happier to think that it has ceased.'

I remain silent refusing to contemplate such an argument.

'Surely it is better,' she continues, 'to think that Papa is now with Christ rather than his agony being prolonged.'

Somehow I manage a smile.

'Come now,' I say, 'you must have faith and share my conviction that your father will be found.'

From the beginning we have always spoken this way, the conciliatory – *your* father – never *my* husband whom I have pledged my soul to discover alive, alive.

Instead of drawing solace from my entreaty as any

dutiful loving daughter would, she flinches and begins to pace the room, thinking only of herself, the shiny landau drawn by six plumed bays, the bride and groom exquisitely attired farewelling a cheering crowd, the honeymoon, a walking tour of the Lakes, boating parties on Windermere.

She stands by the window. I can see her wipe away a furtive tear.

Then she rounds on me.

'How can you insist on this,' she cries. 'When everyone knows – my father—'

Eleanor falters, unable to say it. She stamps her foot in that pretty way which again reminds me of her mother, book in hand, rapping her knuckles on the table for silence, for all in the lecture room to turn enraptured as she makes yet another triumphant, indisputable point.

'How would you feel,' I retort, 'if you forced me to abandon my efforts. Wouldn't you forever be asking yourself if the ships had gone out – what might have been the result, would the face of things have been changed?'

'What might have been the result?' she asks.

'Do you not listen to the Sunday services,' I am beseeching her now, 'the public prayers for all those absent in the Arctic held in sixty churches where the lost men's relatives are known to worship? Don't you see the groundswell of public emotion mounting – money and subscriptions soon pouring in from all over the country?'

Eleanor takes a deep breath, a very portrait of composure. She brushes a speck of dust from her sleeve.

'Very well,' she murmurs. 'I have no choice but to contact Papa's solicitor. From now on, Mr Henry Sellwood will deal with the matter.'

She turns on her heel and makes for the door, slamming it behind her with all her might.

I lie still in the echoing room, my heart pounds fit to bursting. I place my fingers against my throat and feel the beat of blood wildly surging. Only Eleanor has the power to reduce me to this. Several drops of laudanum would calm, but I must be up, coiffed, corseted, impeccably dressed. I am expecting Mr Forsyth, who has volunteered his services gratis to command any vessel I have at his disposal.

In order to charm, I must maintain a stately demeanour, a queenly resolve, instruct him to venture further south than ever before, explore the Great Fish River, keeping to myself the correspondence with Coppin, the ghostly apparitions of Weesy, his daughter.

Yet here I remain, unable to rise, tears silently spilling down a foolish swollen old face.

Poor Netty – what a task she has, how her hands will fly shocked to her mouth. I will submit to my maid, artful conjurer of rouge, gum and pearl powder, and soon Sophy will be at my side, admiring the transformation in the looking glass.

At any mention of Eleanor she will set her lips into a thin line. 'Oh, her,' she will sigh. 'She has always hated you, you know.'

And I will revel in the kisses planted on my forehead, the strong capable fingers easing knotted tendons at the nape of my neck.

Strange to think that the girl's mother and I had once been friends.

Although I can't say I first warmed to the learned authoress of the *Veils*, her celebrated epic verse of some sixteen thousand words.

After twenty-five years, vividly I see Anne Porden still. Hear that gleeful animated voice.

After first being introduced at one Royal Institution lecture she leaned over and offered her autograph, graciously penned some Greek and several phrases of her own poetry on a gold-embossed card, while her father stood over her, prompting and encouraging, not a little vain of his daughter's talents.

Cœur de Lion, she explained. I've been working on it for months. Project Dicky.

It was through a party invitation from my new acquaintance Anne Porden that I first met my future husband. Her cantos, *The Arctic Expeditions*, had so inspired Lieutenant John Franklin as he was then that he contrived an introduction to the author once he returned victorious from his first Canadian overland expedition.

There he stood leaning by the fireplace, seeming too big and wide for his tight-buttoned uniform. He could not take his eyes from his hostess as graciously she flitted from guest to guest.

My companion having not yet arrived, I was able to survey the gathering at my leisure.

Franklin looked a little lost flanked as he was by two raffish rhymers Boz and Flan, who showed no curiosity towards the acclaimed Arctic explorer. Sparred flashes of wit instead like medieval jousters. Although anyone could tell from the undigested literary tone of the banter that their contest was no more than an affectation, an amateur performance studiously learned at home.

Mr Boz and Mr Flan did not converse so much as bat erudite quotations back and forth, plucking witty epigrams from the usual canon, Voltaire, Montaigne,

Milton, Donne, on occasions de Sade if they were feeling particularly risqué, making each observation their own, which made me suspect they had plundered some anthology and were reciting by rote.

Watching Franklin's baffled gaze as he turned to one and then the other, it struck me that this lieutenant – who had crossed vast uncharted tracks of frozen tundra, who would have starved had he not boiled the leather of his reindeer snow shoes, and was now immortalized by the press as *the man who ate his boots* – needed rescue at once.

I noticed he was not the only polar guest cast adrift in Miss Porden's cramped parlour – she now collected discovery heroes for her weekly salons – his colleague Captain Parry, tall, fine-looking, hemmed by a blushing gaggle of admirers, and at the far end of the room, Captain Beechey, a prim man, rather silent and sad.

As I advanced through the crowd, the lieutenant glanced my way with a hopeful expression. Flan gave a low bow.

'Why how delightful, Miss Griffin,' he sneered, raising my hand to his lips, 'we were just remarking that one must be possessed of the Devil to succeed in any of the arts.'

At the mention of the Devil, Franklin frowned and

set his glass on the mantelpiece. He had not touched a drop.

'But, Miss Griffin, I forget,' Flan continued. 'You are a rationalist, unlike us deluded bards of passion and of mirth.'

Boz sidled close and plucked at my sleeve. 'Have you seen him,' he whispered. 'Anne is a genius. Over there by the door.'

'Captain Beechey?' I enquired.

'No,' came the exasperated reply, 'the gentleman hovering beside the young lady trying to converse with the captain. Mr Boz, give Miss Griffin a clue.'

'*So when four years were wholly finished,*' Boz began sotto voce –

She threw her royal robes away.

Make me a cottage in the vale, she said,

Where I may mourn and pray.'

Peering towards the group, the lieutenant coughed.

'Soon to be my nephew, I believe,' he said. 'Forget his name, but he has his eye on my sister's daughter all right.'

'Not Tennyson.'

Boz and Flan rounded on him.

'Not *the* Alfred Tennyson.'

'Yes, that's the one,' he replied and scowled at the dapper man stifling a yawn as Captain Beechey brightened and leaned towards his pretty companion.

Snatching this piece of gossip, the literary fawns rushed across to their hostess – *darling Miss Porden, you'll never guess* – leaving Franklin and me alone.

We were both shy, I incapable of asking him a serious question about his expedition and he quite ignorant of London society, admitting he had never been to the opera and did not think he could sit one out.

I smiled, unable to imagine this large bear of a man confined to a flimsy gilt cane chair, the maroon velvet upholstery and gold tasselled drapes of a theatre box, he who had mapped the North through a telescope, fidgeting to adjust an opera glass. No, it was absurd.

'Captain Parry,' he added, 'has been once and does not mean to go again.'

And we laughed.

Parry could not have been more than twenty-three, such gilded youth, golden features, blond hair, smooth complexion. It was hard not to stare.

Extricating himself from the clutches of his entourage, he managed to join us and confided he would soon be venturing north, somewhat against his inclination for he had seen nothing of other regions of the world.

When I protested, he gestured across the room.

'I fancy poor Beechey feels the same.'

Beautiful, self-deprecating Parry bronzed by the

Nordic sun. I could have kissed this captain to taste the frost of winter on his tongue.

A bell was rung for silence. Miss Porden stepped forward. Her raven hair was loosely braided at the nape of her nape. A choker of rubies glittered at her throat. Her dark eyes large and solemn in that clever narrow face, lips painted carmine accentuating the pallor of her skin.

She raised her arms and began:

'*Sail, sail adventurous Barks! Go fearless forth,*

Storm on his glacier-seat the misty North,

Give to mankind the inhospitable zone,

And Britain's trident plant in seas unknown.'

The lieutenant and his captains listened entranced. Never had I seen Anne so radiant, so ravishing. The lieutenant was the first to lead the thunderous applause. Her cheeks flared pink. Sweat filmed her brow. She smiled and curtsied, somehow rammed that persistent cough back into her lungs, shoulders heaving.

Poor, brave Miss Porden.

Thank you, she would respond to my note praising the success of her at home, *for your enquiries regarding my cough. It has been rather troublesome. I believe it to be partly constitutional and would have been mine under any circumstances, but it has been much augmented by reading out loud. The highest medical authorities have continually told me that it is nervous and of no consequence to my general health, indeed that I know by experience, but I am sorry to find that it is a greater annoyance to others than myself accustomed to the sound of it. My dear Miss Griffin there are times it excites an attention, which is sure to increase it.*

I crumpled the missive and threw it the fire. I'm no fool. Anyone could tell she was dying, of course.

The dining room had been cleared for the dances, chairs ranged against the walls.

All night, Anne partnered the lieutenant in endless rounds of waltzes and quadrilles. Only when he went in search of refreshments did she subside exhausted on a settee and retch into her handkerchief. The moment he reappeared she would collect herself, graciously clink a glass of punch against his. A sublime performance, which cost her afterwards, I'm sure, in calomel and bloodletting, frequent physician's calls.

I did not attend their nuptials. At thirty-two I had reached an age when news of a marriage always affected me as their deaths might have done, as something contrary out of the course of nature.

Hour upon hour that night, I tapped my foot to the string quartet's gay rhythms and kept vigil on the double doors swinging open and shut, hope followed by despair at every entrance and exit. *He* Peter Mark

Roget had promised – six o'clock sharp – and begged me save all the dances for him which I did, declining Captain Parry for the fourth time, and the melancholic Beechey, who seemed content to sit silent on the chair next mine, a chilled bottle of hock on a butler's tray at his side.

Mournfully he watched the lieutenant's niece sashay across the floor guided by Tennyson, the precocious poet, a crimson cravat tied with a flourish beneath his chin, his blue-black hair coiffed tight as astrakhan.

I could hardly breathe the fetid air with its stale scent of attar of roses, withered orchids. Outside a steady downpour dashed against the windows. At the very moment when no doubt the lieutenant proposed to his vivacious poetess, I cursed these modern times – age of confinement, forever waiting for something to happen. For Peter Mark, whose name I could barely inscribe in code on the pages of my journal, to stride through the room and find patience personified seated straight and still, a bright smile concealing acute disappointment. Shame on you, Dr Roget.

I stole a glance at Beechey. Imagined him incarcerated in the dark recesses of a frozen ship, striking off days, months, years from his log book, a wife alone and forlorn as any Rapunzel spinning flax into gold from a turreted tower. Perhaps we are the same, I wanted to say. Perhaps your intrepid voyages to the Pole simply mirror our drawing-room world, an exchange of idle gossip, darning a defunct sock, resigning oneself to boredom and making a virtue of endurance and perseverance. How noble and heroic we are. I lifted my glass. Except Captain Beechey dozed insensible, cradling the empty bottle of hock on his lap.

The clock chimed midnight, the witching hour, time to take my leave, kiss cheek to cheek, embrace Miss Porden – so frail, so thin, shoulder blades curved like angel wings, promising to take her on a carriage ride within the week.

As I waited to say goodbye, I overheard a dowager whisper in her daughter's ear – *And Dr Roget too – he's going to be married.*

Dr Roget, she exclaimed.

Indeed, the mother declared. *So don't set your cap at him.*

I felt my colour flare but the candles burned dim and I believe no one noticed – I could learn no further particulars and struggled to recover myself.

Again, I retired to the house in Bedford Square, careful not to wake Papa as I tiptoed upstairs, along the corridor and into my childhood room where I would light a candle and gaze out the window, laughter and footsteps, a rumble of carriage wheels in the street below, the old mulberry creaking against the casement, the ragged outline of chimneys and rooftops speared by cathedral spires tolling the empty hours.

Again, I would open my journal –

March 25 1824
To think that the purest, the most spontaneous and most tenacious feelings that have ever agitated my heart had been blighted from me. Blighted and worn away by the insufficient worthiness of him who was the object of them. The romance of my life is gone – my dreams are vanishing—

Ah, Doctor Roget – I still glimpse you sometimes, hurrying through the arcades of South Molton Street – stooped, hair greying at the temple like poor Sophy – your stride energetic, resolute not to be deflected from the business at hand.

How I adored my ardent philologist, collector of words, chasing meanings and nuances, indefatigable lepidopterist snatching synonyms from the blue gauze air with a butterfly net. Obsessive, compulsive, enthralled like myself with all manner of trivia, facts and details. And who could not fall in love with the inventor of the kaleidoscope?

Roget, veteran parlour-room campaigner, roué,

charmer, twelve years my senior, always fascinating, always single, the founding member of my monthly Book Society devastating with his mordant criticism of the latest novella.

Try as I might, I could not snare you, Roget. Failed to ambush, catch, flypaper, birdline, mine – all you accused me of – decoy, net, mesh, web, lure, gin.

Bullet words. Grapeshot fired from a musket. Aimed straight for the heart.

I will never forget those games we played whiling the tedium of soirées, at homes, masked balls.

Your turn —

Secret.

Poisoned apple.

Trojan horse,

Greek gift.

Honey trap.

And my reply?

Whited sepulchre

Man of straw.

Paper tiger.

Sheep in wolf's clothing.

Scarecrow

Tattie bogle.

Which made Roget laugh and reach for the notebook he always tucked in his breast pocket.

Roget, we are no longer young, you and I, and one morning I shall read of your death in the obituary notices of *The Times*. Or you of mine – ah what memories, Adieu, we shall sigh.

The *Erebus*. 1847.

November – month of capons and chestnuts

In the beginning, there was game in plenty to be had yet the officers insisted on preserved rations. Complained that seal blood constipates and whale skin gave them diarrhoea despite my entreaties that bear was passable with a taste akin to lamp oil *yet nonetheless good*, that whale could be sliced like mature cheese, with a flavour of ripe chestnuts, that venison was more succulent than the rarest of beefsteaks, the paunch in particular with its bittersweet aftertaste of sorrel. And should one of the crew chance on a seal, I had an endless repertoire of culinary inventions – braised brains and entrails, stuffed shoulder, roast spine tender as turkey breasts; and my favourite, baby seal poached in its mother's milk.

The esteemed proprietor of the Mayfair Grosvenor

Club once flattered me by declaring that a man who devises a new dish is a benefactor to the entire human race. But here in these monstrous hulks there was no one who cared or would listen.

The gross diet of the polar region no more, officer Fitzjames would cry. What, the flower of the British navy reduced to the level of Esquimaux savages? So they encouraged the crew to adhere to salt junk and hard tack, and in my opinion set a sorry example to their men who when the season permitted were allowed to kill only for sport.

In the mess room, Fitzjames slams down his glass. 'Damn you, Canot, bring me the charts.'

Each day in the company of Lieutenants Gore, Fairholme, Tutt and Des Voeux, he maps the disconsolate escarpments, frozen levels and granite beachscapes.

Already he has named the hummocks and floes after prince consorts, politicians, courtiers, friends.

Even when the ravaged pinnacles of his empire fall, he replots the transformed vistas: Melbourne Straits, Sandwich Bay, Mount Nelson.

This new Britannia. Cartographer's dream.

It is hard now to describe how happy the officers felt at the onset of the voyage, how determined to be frozen in *just one winter*. For weeks we dodged about – to borrow a whaling phrase – pools of water off Cape Warrender. The nights were becoming shorter. Each setting sun blazed more fiercely encircled by red mists as the light dimmed. Against the skyline, stars swung in long curves like the sweep of a goshawk.

'I wish I could write to the relations of each and every one on board,' Sir John Franklin declared after one evening's entertainment in the great cabin, leading the toast to sweethearts and wives, 'and assure them of the happiness I feel in my officers, my crew, and my ship.'

Speed, our commander called for speed. From the quarterdeck he gave orders to let out more canvas. And willingly the officers gave in to the 'old gentleman' as they called him, admired his fighting spirit, his reckless abandonment in steering Her Majesty's ships through narrow channels, those siren songs from slender floes, calling up to the ice-master in the crow's nest, enthused by cheers of 'farthest north'.

Icebergs ahead, astern. Icebergs to port and starboard. You can imagine how we Arctic novices crammed the bows before this ocean of impressions – like travellers arriving in a strange town, threading uncertain paths through marble pillars and colonnades, fantastical white palaces and Italianate cities; there an island carved with creeks and bays or the emerald entrance to an immense cavern which the sea filled with foam; the everlasting snow, a perpetual flood ambered into place. Words were lost, inaudible.

As for myself, gazing at sapphire perpendicular cliffs, so perfectly even and marked in a glitter of separate galleries that to my shame an image rose in my mind of the Palm House at Kew. You could say metaphors failed us.

In the beginning, the officers actually believed that to return to the place we called home with nothing to show, without a passage, would be more painful than dying itself.

Home – the streets of Piccadilly and Pigalle illuminated with the spermaceti of whales, which during the night, I have seen in their hundreds close to the rocks of a summer lagoon feeding on young coal fish. Home – snow perhaps falling in swift festive flurries and women promenading the boulevards, waists cinched tight with baleen corsets, their perfume fixed in ambergris.

That first summer of 1845 was the mildest on Admiralty records. Guided by favourable winds, our ships skimmed the shores like migrating swallows and reached Lancaster Sound in less than a month. As we entered Davis Strait, an icecap at least one mile high sent ceaseless gales roaring out to sea. At nightfall the cap glowed green then faded to grey like a living creature passing into death.

The crew saw it as a premonition, augured worse than setting sail on a Friday, they said.

Strange to think back – the Esquimaux we encountered at Baffin Bay took our vessels for creatures with wings and asked what kind of ice paned the skylights. If only that were so and we could soar on the back of the north wind.

Still we pushed through widening waters past Cape Riley and sought a winter harbour on the lee side of Beechey Island.

A time of recreation and skating frolics when we scrambled merrily over glaciers and murdered migrating geese and auks in the white glare of our day-midnight, those smooth distant grounds on which we played football and where Fitzjames shot our first bear.

The cold came upon us gradually. First the freezing of our water casks, cases of claret, cognac. Then the salt beef turned to Venetian mosaic, sugar to cork, flour much the same. Our precious preserved meats to cannonballs. With crowbar and axe, chisel and mallet I prepared the flinty meals. Best to smash the barrels with the meats, stow beneath the galley, allow one day to thaw.

We luxuriated in ices of course – sugared cranberries, scalding water and a knob of butter gave a fair imitation of an impromptu strawberry glacé and you had to handle a spoon deftly before it fastened to your tongue.

Our first Christmas, a sparkling night of sleigh bells, songs and glad communing of hearts in faraway lands, when we drank a moiety of our Heidsieck and the opening leads of the solstice piled into hummocks on our port beam. No harm done.

The following spring, creeping from the polar night, blood coursed our veins. After a dark season of torpor, it was as if we had all stuttered into life like toys in a doll's house, endlessly arranged and reconfigured by the busy fingers of a child.

How can I describe the rise of the sun after eight months of utter darkness, a spiral ray of Italianate pink shoots from the horizon increasing in brilliance like a flame dancing through a blowpipe, the whole eastern sky incarnadined with tints of rose, green and indigo until the entire brimming disc reveals itself and burnishes the blanched compass of our world.

Then all too soon, the vision fades, gone as swiftly as a whale rolling over and made doubly desolate after a heavy fall of snow.

Keenly we waited for a dormant sea to arise and sniff

the briny air, open waters to flash teal and cobalt between receding floes, islands ablaze with dog lichen, vivid scatterings of yellow poppies and cream white flowers among coarse marshes lining the shore, fragments of whalebone and driftwood surfacing from the mud.

All of us, I think, craved to be freed, for the constellations to tilt on their summer axis and the seasons to resume their order in this most unnatural place. We had endured. We had been throttled, squeezed, jammed, tossed and tumbled about, nipped and pressed. We had pumped a leaking ship for an entire winter, kept her habitable, made life aboard 'fair tolerable', as the officers would say.

And now we insisted on our reward, the wretched glacier *would* thaw to a frenzied whirl of summer migrations, a tribe of Esquimaux setting up camp perhaps.

Black guillemots arrived and set off quickly, laying their eggs and urging the offspring into the air within four or five weeks. One morning, an offshore breeze raked great windrows of eider feathers across the skies, sent them dense and whirling floating by, a theatrical snowstorm that not even our impresario Charles Dickens could have devised. Some caught in the rim of the old gentleman's black bicorne hat as moodily he strode the deck, desperate to be off, rounding on those still aiming their pistols at green-winged gulls – no time, you fools, for that.

Put it this way, our swift release from Beechey Island beguiled us like a mirage. Blessed with propitious winds, the unfamiliarity of balmy weather swelled our skin. I watched our encampment from Beechey's cove recede, those blank slopes marked with graves – three young men who died quite suddenly within months – John Torrington, stoker, New Year's Eve, John Hartnell, able seaman, three days later, and William Braine, marine, April 3, 1846.

Post-mortems revealed blackened lungs, tuberculosis and two advanced cases of Signor Gonorrhoea. Think nothing of it.

Yet those stark headstones rose from the shingles, accusing as a portent.

Choose ye this day whom ye will serve.

Within a month, our vessels had rounded Cape Walker, the last headland marked positively on the map and we nudged unknown waters. A strait which the previous season whalers had reported invisible, walled over, impassable with ice, now beckoned, shining lapis luring us due south. Franklin gave orders to press on –

the weather too fine to waste laying caches or messages, no time for that.

The lookout sent down the cry – *King William Land lying immediately to the south.*

I ran sweating from the galley, and a film of ice tightened my skin like a mask.

An ebony slouch of rock; glacier-streaked, vertebrae of snow, bone white along its crest.

'Mr Reid,' Franklin called to the ice-master buffeted by sheets of sleet whipping through the rigging. 'By our estimates, King William Land stands from the North American mainland at a distance of two hundred miles. The very portal of the Passage, are we not?'

The ice-master remained silent.

Fitzjames tried to rally the men into a cheer. But their response was sullen, half-hearted.

'In a week, perhaps two, we'll push through,' he cried.

As the ships hove to, Franklin's second in command was piped aboard. Crozier had a rough sallow look as if he had been hard at the grog since we weighed anchor from Beechey's shores.

He strode towards the officers and saluted Franklin.

'With the pack ice still melting and scored with open leads –' Fitzjames began, oblivious to the severity of Crozier's countenance.

'With the weather near perfect,' he continued, 'and two years' provisions, the steam engines functioning flawlessly, we have every confidence, sir, in bulling our way through to the mainland for our Queen and country.'

Hands clenched behind his back, Crozier surveyed the pitiless channels ahead.

'Mr Fitzjames,' Crozier eyed the young officer with distaste, 'one of the most stunning features of an Arctic summer is its abrupt end, sometimes overnight. In late August, conditions could change at any time.'

Baffled into silence, Fitzjames glanced at his commander for help.

Crozier took a step towards him.

'Overestimate the season, by a week or even a day and you expect to spend ten months locked in a moving wasteland, which could crush a single ship within twenty-four hours.'

Fitzjames collected himself by straightening his cuffs, tried to appease Crozier with a handsome honest smile.

'We await your counsel, sir,' he said in the concilia-tory voice for which he had been trained.

Crozier shook his head and sighed.

'What do you say, Mr Reid,' he shouted to the ice-master. 'Use the weather that's left to find safe anchorage, winter over and renew the attempt next year?'

'Yes, sir,' came the reply.

Sir John Franklin held up one hand.

'God has guided us this far.'

He stood gazing skyward as if awaiting an answer.

'Lay steam on,' he called.

August 22, 1846 – the ships entered the pack.

Three tons of coal a day just to keep steam in the boilers became the purser's anxious refrain as we followed serpentine leads, the ships repeatedly backing and grinding full power ahead.

Fitzjames officially named the slender opening Peel Sound to a fanfare of trumpets and did his best to ignore Crozier's dour predictions uttered in his fierce Ulster drawl.

'Quite literally, we stand at a point of no return,' Crozier announced when once again the vessels hove to – 'with only two options.'

He glared at the officers with a ferocious expression.

'How so, Mr Crozier?' Fitzjames asked giving a curt bow.

'We can continue this assault on the ice and expend fuel at a prodigious rate,' he replied, 'perhaps force a passage to the mainland before they close completely.

Or we can turn back at once and get out of the ice before we are caught in its maw.'

Crozier fixed the young man with such an accusing look that he flushed and retreated to the forrard rail.

'That is – if it is not too late, of course.'

At this Fitzjames rounded on him.

'Mr Crozier, sir, forcing the passage has been a race after all,' the officer began. 'To quit the run halfway is clearly not the way to win. As Mr Reid has again indicated – ' he gave an impatient gesture towards the crow's nest – 'open leads are still visible to the west, precisely the direction in which we wish to go.'

'Then perhaps, Mr Fitzjames, you might consider the most shocking course of all,' Crozier retorted, the wind shrieking at his back. 'Abandon one ship, load coal in the other and press forward at full speed. Not to win the passage,' he smiled, 'but to outwit winter and escape the pack at all costs.'

It was then that Franklin ascended from his cabin to the quarterdeck.

'We will practise the principles of patience and perseverance,' he addressed his officers. 'Come now, Mr Crozier, it has worked for me before in 1818 in the *Dorothea*.'

He beckoned Fitzjames. 'Draw the boiler fires and

let steam down,' he called. 'We will warp our way through.'

He dismissed Crozier with a gracious wave. 'Time, sir, to return to your ship.'

Crozier managed a half-hearted salute and without a word marched to the waist.

All week, fatigue parties armed with saws, picks, axes and chisels smashed the closing leads, the remaining crew set kedge anchors in the fast ice and winched the vessels a ship's length at a time.

It was a sickening sensation to feel the decks quiver beneath one's feet, the great beams buckling with a noise of heavy gunfire.

All hands at the capstan.

From morning to night, the men heaved on the ropes – the rough twine chafing their shoulders – dragging the ships no further than several yards a day north-west of this shore called King William Land. There was something obscene in our pitiful progress, the sheer waste of effort, chipping and scraping an unending surface reaching to nowhere, towards a promise of a passage which might not exist.

We all hated Franklin and the officers then. Their boyish cries of wonder, the senseless instructions shouted from the quarterdeck.

Sir John's incessant prayers grated the most, not

loud proclamations, but uttered fiercely beneath his breath as if he and his God were locked in dispute as to the exact terms of their contract.

Crozier no longer communicated with the *Erebus*. Instead he remained by the *Terror*'s helm and watched the blinding white channels blink and seal shut.

Rumours ran among the crew that we were caught in the unmelting glaciers of the Beaufort stream pouring from the polar cap and when the sun vanished it would splinter our vessels like a pair of crackers teasing out a walnut.

Bedford Square. June 1850.

The wrist on my right hand is swollen and aches with writing – Captains Ross and Richardson commanding the Admiralty ships the *Investigator* and the *Enterprise* sailed into Deptford without finding a trace of the lost expedition. Not a relic, not a word, nothing but geography to report.

So seated at the escritoire in my Japan Room, I continue with the petitions.

To Zachary Taylor, President of the United States, careful in my choice of phrasing – *yet I should rejoice that it was to America we owed our restored happiness*; to the Tsar of Russia, pleading a search operation mounted through Bering Strait and the coast of Siberia; to John Rae of the Hudson's Bay Company, expressing my utmost confidence in his ability and perseverance to do what few other men could accomplish, adding *I do not know whether you consider that the mouth of the Great*

Fish River be examined; to the Admiralty, about the purchase of two dockyard lighters – *I cannot attempt to conceal from the Board that it is only by the sacrifice of all my private property and by the additional aid of borrowed capital that I shall be able to effect my object*; should I receive no reply or reassurance from the above, to the wealthy Silas Burrows of New York wondering *if he thought I might be able to procure a few thousand pounds to add to my own, so as to enable me to send a small vessel or two vessels with boats to those especial parts where I am persuaded the lost ships and crews are most likely to be found*; and lastly to my husband – *I do not let the Admiralty rest about you although they do not do all I desire.*

When finally I set down my blunted quill, I reread my missive which Captain Ross returned sealed, unopened – *I try to prepare myself for every trial which may be in store for me, but dearest, if you ever open this, it will be I trust because I have been spared the greatest trial of all.*

I glance out of the window. Another season swings on its hinges. A robin I have been feeding crumbs all winter flits back and forth along the sill dancing across a patch of sunlight. Aware I am watching he even has the temerity to tap his beak on the pane. June – month of hope and propitious winds, the mulberry now in its full flush of crimson and fronds of white lilac appearing in the garden square below.

Franklin, I dreamed of you last night and stretching out on the rumpled sheets of this empty bed, I remembered you were no longer at my side.

I was too tired to be awake. There is much to be done and I am alone now.

Again I was tempted – reached for the phial. When I am sad, I seek solace in laudanum. I am very often sad, Franklin, although to you I would appear reckless, five long years since I've heard the sound of your voice.

No need for that, Jane, you would whisper, taking me in your arms. You must not overexcite your mind with any gossip you might hear at Government House.

Anne haunted my dreams and once again I found myself asking if you loved me as much as you had loved her, a hard question and tedious of me to persist.

I remember on the eve of your second Canadian overland expedition, 15th of February 1825 – how proud Anne had been of Captain Franklin's promotion – I called round with some gifts, fur-lined gloves, a silver pencil, the Diamond miniature edition of Shakespeare. I found the candlelit hallway echoing with the sound of whispering, Anne's sister comforted by a group of relations, a priest waiting to take the sacrament and read the chapter from the Corinthians. I set down my presents and prepared to take my leave, when the sister rose and bade me visit my friend.

'She would want to see you,' she murmured ushering me up the stairs and pushing open the door.

Anne was lying on the sofa before a fierce fire blazing in the grate. A physician stood at her side. Leeches squirmed between his tweezers as he laid them along her extended arm. Nearby baby Eleanor kicked and gurgled from her wicker cradle.

At my approach, Anne smiled and with her free hand plucked a silk Union Jack she had embroidered for your journey. Leaning over to admire it, I looked away. Then gently so she wouldn't see, I tried to fold the bloodstained flag.

Blood everywhere, dripping from her wrist, splashing onto the carpet, expelled in huge racking sobs from her mouth.

'I am far from well today,' she managed to say beneath her breath.

I mopped her brow, held a spittoon to cracked lips, sat with her into the night. You had been detained at Deptford supervising the ships. Four days later Anne died as they lifted her from the sofa to the bed. After the funeral her sister, Mrs Kay, sent me a pair of her white kid gloves and a garnet and pearl brooch containing a dark lock of hair.

In your absence, London society was hard on the famous explorer – I had to defend you at one of the Book Society meetings. As we gathered in the lecture hall of the Royal Institution, Disraeli was the first to declare that the day after Anne's funeral, a letter had arrived in which Captain Franklin expressed his good spirits, his satisfaction at the excellent appointment of his vessel, saw every prospect of the expedition's success and hopes of his wife's recovery.

'Do you mean to say he had not been awake to the poor woman's wretched condition?' This from Roget, who glanced my way.

I willed myself to remain silent, took my place at the table and flicked through our chosen novel, *Melmoth the Wanderer*.

'Ambition surely disgraces a man,' Disraeli opined. 'For who chooses to part from his wife on her deathbed?'

All at once, I found all eyes of the group on mine.

'What do you think, Jane? Weren't you present at her final hour?'

Roget again.

I closed the book and rose to my feet.

'Shame on you,' I said. 'How can you pander to such idle and contradictory gossip? It was Anne's decided wish that Captain Franklin should not delay in going and she told me quite certainly that the circumstance of his departure had not hastened the crisis of her complaint.'

Roget stretched out his legs and smiled.

'Before he sailed and at Anne's insistence,' I continued, my voice beginning to tremble with agitation, 'he was obliged to settle all his affairs as if his wife would never recover and he himself would not return.'

Roget stared at me with an expression of wry amusement. I blushed for I had not intended to say so much.

When you returned on the 10th of November 1827, triumphant, feted, soon to be knighted, you called on Bedford Square, and deeply impressed my family by having named a distant cape after us, Point Griffin.

By appointment at four in the afternoon the following week, I went to 55 Devonshire Street, where you and Mrs Kay greeted me warmly.

At first I felt awkward as you led me past the chill, shuttered rooms into the parlour where Anne had held her soirées. Her presence lingered in the elegant Regency furnishings, the walnut cabinets lined with books and journals, her escritoire on which lay a folio of poems bound in blue ribbon.

I wondered what you might have done with her writing. I imagined you sifting through her papers, unable to decide which to keep, which to discard.

I was ushered to a chair by the window. Outside, dark clouds rumbled with thunder. A flash of lightning hissed through the skies.

A maid came through with a tray set with glasses, a decanter of Madeira, ginger biscuits arranged on a plate.

'My dear Miss Griffin, it is always such a pleasure.' You stood before me, a parcel clasped in your hands, gracing me with that shy smile I now miss and know so well. You seemed taller, leaner, more agile and purposeful than the lieutenant I had met at Anne's at home.

Proffering the package, you watched me unwrap the brown paper and open the box – three pairs of slippers made by native Indian women. Finely fashioned seal skin with intricate stitched soles of the softest leather to the touch.

Caribou, you said.

The sister-in-law quietly withdrew into the recesses of the parlour and adjusted the frame of her embroidery, deftly threading a needle with crimson silk. From upstairs, I heard a child cry out and the sound of footsteps hurrying along the corridor.

I had forgotten about the daughter.

Mrs Kay glanced up from her work. 'Poor darling,' she whispered. 'Eleanor has problems sleeping.'

'Could she be brought down?' I asked. 'I would love to see her again.'

'Perhaps another time,' Anne Porden's sister replied.

You took your place opposite mine and we began to talk effortlessly, no mention of opera or parties and London society.

Ceremoniously you unrolled an oiled paper map and traced your finger across the charts to Griffin Point, west of the mouth of the Mackenzie River, among a multitude of other illustrious names, the Duke of Wellington, Lord Nelson, the Prince Consort, the Queen, dear Captain Parry and Beechey.

I felt honoured, indeed nervous. My heart fairly hammered in my chest. I confessed that when he received the news Papa was quite beside himself.

'My dearest Miss Griffin,' you exclaimed, 'the highest object of my desire is to faithfully perform my duty.'

Studying your smiling animated face I would later observe in my journal that this Captain Franklin has a charm of spirit and address. He is sensitive and I have heard it said that whenever he has to cane one of his middies he trembles from head to foot. He runs a tight, honest ship. He is brave and kind, and not without humour. Anne Porden loved him. Adored him. And she was extremely gifted and fastidious, rejecting several proposals of marriage at which others would have leapt. Who would not envy her? Had she lived and been born a man, she might have outstripped Dickens with the mercurial mischief of her pen.

Others less charitable might paint a different portraiture, Franklin, the bluff, solid mariner, ill at ease outside his accustomed officer circle, disturbed by any deviation from his own circumscribed beliefs, doggedly obedient to Admiralty instructions.

Yet that afternoon, as a storm sent rain pelting across the square and I accepted your invitation to attend the distinguished ceremony of your knighthood, I found myself drawn to a certain charisma, a strong personal magnetism. I became flustered, thrilled and flattered in turns.

Point Griffin. I could not tear my gaze from our family name on the map.

Fortune smiled on you. You were famous, a national hero. I had never met a man of action before, polar campaigner, champion of expeditions into uncharted lands. Instead I had been acquainted with scholars, bookish, learned, always ready with a quote, some reference to the classics, witty, erudite, yet always indoors, a fire burning in the grate.

You were describing a moon halo, a great whirling system of luminous concentric circles of colour as if a rainbow were looped around a vast silver coin.

How intently you talked.

I listened enthralled, felt the narrow confines of the parlour expand.

And yes, when you asked, I married you of course.

Sometimes, but not often, I wonder how Anne might have fared in my situation. A dead first wife is a hard act to follow, shadowed as you are by her ghost, etched in the hard defiant features of the daughter. Hating, despising you.

Perhaps she would have vanished into the dream world of her poem *Cœur de Lion*, leaving her husband, unprotected, vulnerable, alone.

Whereas I – well, I have been instrumental, an invisible chess player, steering my husband through appointments and promotions, watching him rise triumphant from knight to governor and now captain and commander. At the same time vigilant in safeguarding my reputation as the submissive obedient wife.

In hindsight, it might be said that you, Franklin, have become my creation, my very own invention.

Mark my words it is my duty to transform you into a hero rivalling Horatio. Indeed I have been petitioning for a column higher than Nelson's. There in Trafalgar Square, you will preside flanked by griffins instead of lions. And perhaps I can exert my influence to prohibit the feeding of pigeons at twopence a bag.

The *Erebus*. 1847.

December – month of mulled wine and brandy-buttered mince pies

Beyond our encampment, the storehouses, the carpenter's shop, the blacksmith's forge, beyond the observatory and lookout tower, a raised plot of frozen graves encircled by stones. There we have read the service of the burial of the dead, repeated the Lord's Prayer, sprinkled snow for dust before sealing the catafalque we had crudely fashioned to admit the rows of coffins and bid adieu to our fourteen comrades laid out in their narrow dwellings; Sir John Franklin, the old gentleman, the second sombre count, this sorrowful year 1847, June 11.

I trace a path across the unmelting scalloped plains towards the gothic turreted outlines of my Rouen.

Poor Tutt still slaves at his fractured jumble. He

pants and leans on his spade, quite spent from his efforts. Feigns not to notice my approach. Bad sport that he is.

Even though every muscle in my body aches and my swollen fingers blister against the coarse stitching of my gloves, I rejoice in this work, chipping blocks of masonry hard as anthracite. Take a childish pleasure in the way fresh water fetched from the fire hole seals each slab fast like cement.

I swing the ice pick and revel in the echoing ring of shattered glass as if I had smashed a thousand plates at a Greek banquet. The racket of my industry and perhaps my tuneless whistle irritates Tutt, I can tell, from the way his thin shoulders stiffen, and the racking cough suddenly seems the strongest part of himself.

Soon afterwards, Tutt gathers his gear and limps off. I pity him. Should offer to help, get him started at least. But these lieutenants, proud upright men, have arrived with the Union Jack folded in their valises together with their arrogance and reserve, the decorated uniforms they once changed into every night when summoned to dine in the great cabin.

Once a warrant officer always a warrant officer, was how Osmer introduced himself explaining that the steward is the last on board covered by the Captain's

Instructions *to have charge of the steep pot and place meat into it and be responsible for any part, which shall be lost through his want of care.*

Yet what a sight met my eye when my assistant Coffin laid Goldner's provisions on the counters, watery slabs of bully beef, veal and mutton much the same, brine-soaked vegetables fibrous in texture. Coffin almost mutilated his fingers hammering away at the tins, trying to open the damn things, each can exhaling an odorous puff like a last mortal breath.

The meat had more horseflesh than I was used to preparing – weighed with bone, offal, even gravel, the soups largely water thickened with alum.

Canot, who prides himself on premium ingredients, market fare always in season, each month a choice yield, could see that the Admiralty's supplier had turned every trick, so to speak.

In layman's terms, I could have explained that to procure such quantities of produce for early spring, you had to rely on the gleanings of autumn kill, none prime and fresh, but six months old, salted and decomposing, or winter-weakened animals driven on the hoof.

Why, I could have held a series of evening lectures on the subject, supplies tampered with the leavings of second-hand butchers' shops, tanneries and slaughter-houses.

From the rust iron odour of the congealed fare, I could have described in considerable detail how an animal slaughtered quickly and cruelly by which I mean *sloppily* covers his entire hide with excrement; that his terror can dull a quarter of beef slapped beneath a greasy cleaver.

And the wastage; the tins themselves ruptured, gas escaping coarse soldered seams until the drums burst.

But I decided not to mention any of this to Osmer, who took any criticism as a personal affront.

With considerable ingenuity from these sorry ingredients, I would fashion a rich ragout flavoured with crushed thyme and cognac and might cheat with chicken stock boiled from the last batch of fowl to concoct a tolerable mock-turtle soup.

'Excellent,' Sir John Franklin would murmur, lifting a spoon to his lips. 'Your secret, Canot?'

'A dash of Devonshire cream, sir.'

Soon all the officers were pronouncing the provisions top quality and the banquets held in the great cabin proved an unqualified success.

By then I had Coffin, smart in his page's uniform, tend to the wines, and deft and promising he had been, a starched serviette draped over one arm.

Until opening the salt pork, I reeled from a putrid mess of pickled cheeks, ears, offal – everything, as I later complained to Osmer, except *the squeal*. 'Just a heap of bones, scrag-ends, souse and hog's feet.'

Against his protestations, the menacing references to the captain's standing orders, I finally had my way. Had forty stinking containers of the stuff thrown out – quite a performance, which required endless inspections, Sir John Franklin's official declaration that these stores were unusable, all stamped approved and signed by three officers in a report to be dispatched to Admiralty House.

So began the cairn, our first winter on Beechey Island, which someone might find one day – I hope.

Most mornings, Coffin sets down a tray outside Osmer's locked door. I try to encourage the purser with scrambled eggs whisked from the last of the powder, strong brews of tea laced with brandy. I am fond of the man, I suppose, and miss our games of chess. The way he used to announce *checkmate* with a decisive click of his tongue.

At six bells, supper will be served.

First I take our commander his antiscorbutic cordial. The elegant flutes of olive oil and lime juice no more. The detested stocks of sauerkraut and raw potato run down to six tubs.

Instead I resort to beer fermented with the remnants of dried peaches, raisins, barley and brown sugar, which the men drink in the most liberal quantities.

Crozier sits at the oak desk in the arctic bureau of the great cabin tirelessly scratching indecipherable missives to the Admiralty. What's the use?

I place the cordial beside him. Bearded, ginger-haired, Crozier eyes me with the same expression of bored hostility as the Highland bulls mired in the peat paddocks of Stromness.

Our commander seldom alludes to his former captain – finds it hard to forgive him.

'Sir John Franklin,' he once declared, 'desired above all to be everyone's friend, their best chum. His avuncular easygoing style was more suited to an ambassadorial life in a governor's mansion and represented the one kind of authority loathed by the crew, the slack captain with a joke on his lips and a gentle hand.

'He had forgotten how lonely it can be – a very hermit's life, with no congenial spirit you can talk to except to kick up a row with the helmsman or abuse you, Canot.'

He glanced my way and smiled.

'Does the irony not escape you,' he asked, 'that Franklin died in his sleep?'

The curtains hang heavy against the great stern

window carved across the transom, the hems mottled and wet. Crozier leans back in his chair enveloped in clouds of vapour.

The papers held in his fox-fur mittens steam and I notice that the fresh ink has begun to run in rivulets reminding me of tears, kohl streaking a courtesan's perfectly painted face.

'Keep it to yourself, Canot,' he says in his hoarse Irish brogue. 'Not yet told the men of my intention. But a spring evacuation it is.'

The commander's illegible scrawl fades to a faint blur misting the page. He crumples the document and tosses it among the sodden pile strewn at his feet.

Spring – who believes in such a thing?

'Spirit room, Canot,' Crozier murmurs. 'You know what I want.'

Ever the professional, I have arrived prepared of course – I know our captain better than his seasoned officers – and on cue, whip out a brandy bottle from beneath the folds of my astrakhan cloak and place it beside him.

He motions me to an overstuffed chair as I fill his glass. 'I prefer to stand, sir,' I say, knowing that the silk upholstery will be soaked and I can't afford its flaying sting when I go up on deck to deliver the lookout's broth.

'Of course, Canot,' Crozier whispers. 'I've always liked a man who is in earnest.'

As Crozier cradles his tumbler and takes shaky sip after sip, I wait for the familiar exhalation of breath, pensive prelude to narratives I have heard before. This being our second winter, we know one another's stories by rote and take malicious pleasure in correcting each other when recounting them. We heckle and interrupt, point out deliberate exaggerations and omissions – it's become quite a sport with us.

Crozier, Franklin's second in command, we spare of course – reluctant hero – nerves shot to pieces on raw liquor. Mechanically, as if in a dream, he steels himself to steer us towards the secret of how all this will end.

Outside, the ice begins its nocturnal growl, snuffling around the hull in a low thrumming bass. At a rattle of china in the dresser, Crozier instinctively reaches out to steady his glass. This evening, the uneven vibration of the pack sends shudders through stout oak planking, the soles of my leather boots, my woollen-stockinged feet, quickens my tired beating heart. But we ignore it, of course. Pretend nothing is amiss in the guttering candlelight, sheathes of papers swept to the floor and a constant pounding at the doors as if some dear lace-capped dame had unwittingly summoned to her drawing room a host of poltergeists from a ouija board.

'Stay and take a nightcap, Canot,' Crozier says above a thin whistling hum like countless arrows in flight.

I pour us both a measure. I must ask what to do about my boy Coffin, restless insomniac pacing the lower decks. Coffin wide-eyed and insistent that his enemies intend to spray him with acid – can hear them drilling the bare partition behind his bunk.

Before I can devise a way of broaching the subject, Crozier nods to himself slowly and his massive shoulders droop as he lets out a sigh.

'Did I ever tell you, Canot, there was a ball,' he smiles, 'here on these ships – this very cabin illuminated with chandeliers and perfumed with bouquets of wild yellow flowers, great sprigs of the stuff which the good folk of Hobart brought in. Wattle they called it.'

All at once an image stirs in my mind of the South of France, hamlets of stone and terracotta tiles deserted at the siesta hour, the palpitating heat of midsummer when shutters are drawn to the shrill of cicadas and carried in the rustle of a breeze a sharp citrus scent dusting the air with pollen.

'Mimosa,' I say.

Puzzled, Crozier glances my way.

'French for wattle, sir.'

'Ah, mimosa, I like that,' Crozier murmurs savouring the word. 'The *Erebus* was beautifully fitted up for the dancing,' he continues, undaunted by a great hammering reverberating from the upper decks, 'and reflected the greatest ingenuity and taste on the part of Lieutenant Bird who proved the most active officer on that occasion. Dead now, of course.'

I can hear those dour lamentations still – thus says the Lord of Hosts – sacred to the memory of – and my own private bitter prayer – *we have sown much and harvested little, we eat but never have enough; we drink but never have our fill; we clothe ourselves but no one is warm.* Bird was a man eight feet tall, his cloak streamed in the wind. He was a raven beating ebony wings.

No I do not wish to think of Bird or the others now.

I concentrate on Crozier instead. In the half-light, our commander shifts his weight on the leather horsehair chair, one hand still clamped on his tumbler. An inch of brandy tilts back and forth against the frosted glass etched with the billowing sails of Elizabethan galleons.

'Imagine,' he says, 'these ships moored head to stern in the sheltered cove of the Government Domain, pale tides lacing the shore, waters calm as a lake.'

At this our ice queen screeches and rages in the most obscene and highest soprano.

'Ten years of Discovery Service and now dispatched

to the unknown regions of Antarctica – you can understand that I, no longer a young man, keenly anticipated this diversion at Hobart Town laid out like a miniature village in the shadows of Mount Wellington.'

Outside, strange weening cries, punctuated at intervals with sharp twangs like bow strings.

I picture our commander attired in swallow-breasted gold and blue alert at the ship's rail. He salutes as the British flag is hoisted from the sentry box, promising a week's reprieve from the next feat of endurance.

Crozier describes a day of dazzling light, and in the main square, a semicircle of chestnut trees white and showy in full candle bloom. At first, he was struck by the gaiety of the scene, the paved streets and neat sandstone warehouses, scarlet geraniums spilling from tubs on the windowsills. The wheel of gulls and a brine tang in the clear buoyant air reminded him of Brighton or Leamington Spa.

And there on the wharf, arms outstretched in greeting, stood Sir John Franklin, governor of this remote island outpost – our same 'old gentleman', who by the sword of the young Queen had been knighted and hailed as a hero for completing two Arctic overland missions, devouring reindeer boots on frozen tundras, outwitting mutinies among Indian voyagers.

I know the stories.

His reward – seven landlocked years of penal rule – had not served Franklin well.

'Why,' Crozier, says, refilling his glass, 'Sir John had grown heavy-jowled, a paunch strained the seams of his uniform, and a defeated look dulled his countenance, which was a shock to behold. Yet flanked by Jane, his wife, and Sophy Cracroft, his pretty young niece, Franklin fairly brimmed with joy as he embraced Captain Ross, who would lead our ships further south than any other man.'

Crozier stares into the dark recesses of the great cabin, whorled with shadows cast from a flicker of oil wicks. For a moment the ice growl has ceased. Instead a steady drip of water from the ceiling, which can drive a man insane to listen to for long. Sometimes, I wonder which is worse, those damned high-pitched puppy whines or the constant drizzle of our vessels.

'The niece,' Crozier continues, 'curtsied and extended one kid-gloved hand. Unlike the other ladies, drab in outdated faded crinolines, she was attired at the very height of fashion judging by the expensive cut of her light tulle dress tied tight beneath the breasts.'

He shivers and draws his wolfskin cloak closer. His green eyes soften in that broad blunt honest face.

I pity him, incarcerated on this immovable block of ice.

That first night as the captains dined in the banquet hall of Government House, Sir John Franklin announced he had personally supervised two hundred convicts in the construction of an observatory, specifically for the officers' use, that for weeks he had paced the docks impatient for his guests to arrive, for a sail to appear on the horizon.

Seated opposite Crozier, and resplendent in taffeta and lace, the niece lowered her fan and confided that the observatory had consumed all her uncle's spare time. 'He is so much interested in the subject of terrestrial magnetism,' she whispered, 'that nothing could give him more relaxation.'

An excited murmur from her aunt as she leaned towards Captain Ross – 'Your arrival, sir, has added much to my husband's happiness and it is the general remark in town that Sir John appears to them in a new light, so bustling, frisky and merry with his new companions.'

She lifted her glass – 'It is our intention, sir' – she directed an indulgent smile at the young captain at her side – 'that the new observatory be called Rossbank.'

At this everyone clapped and cheered.

'And I shall commission the portrait artist Thomas

Bock to paint the three of you standing before it, each with your hats off and a bunch of silver wattle in your button hole – I will insist on it.'

Lady Franklin proved indefatigable in the daily entertainments, expeditions to the summit of Mount Wellington, picnics on the verdant slopes of her precious Ancanthe, a Grecian structure fronted with Doric columns from which she hoped to found a Royal Society for the Advancement of Science. Crozier observed that one could not help but pay court to this formidable lady as she reclined on a cashmere rug shaded by the Palladian porticos of her folly elaborating such plans for her empire – a botanical garden and natural history museum – she would persuade her husband to inaugurate an annual regatta and found a proper secondary school. As for the Female Convict Factory – why, the girls remain imbecile and idle, she declaimed, they must be made to pick oakum for Her Majesty's ships and their own moral good.

'I would love,' Lady Franklin once announced, leading her party through a rustle of blue gums fringing Ancanthe, 'to get rid of the harsh, awkward name of Van Diemen and the expletive *land* altogether, and replace it with that of Tasmania, which is perfectly familiar to us and gaining ground every day in writing.'

She turned and shot her entranced guests a triumphant look, the solemn-eyed niece in particular who hung on her every word. 'Should I not succeed,' she continued, lifting her skirts above the dusty rutted track, 'I would humbly plead that the name Diemenia be substituted. I'd also prefer Hobart rather than Hobart Town, but one is obliged to trim as other politicians do and give up something in order to gain the rest if my reasoning is to be of no avail.'

Captain Ross and Sir John Franklin thrilled with their daily calculations from the observatory, the routine examinations of the ships – interrogations with the crew – and showed little interest in pleasure trips to mountains and valleys, the botanizing of butterflies and orchids. Always the niece claimed Crozier as her partner among the audience before which Lady Franklin performed. And he was flattered by the company of this demure pretty girl, parasol twined in one slender hand, so proud and eagerly attentive to her aunt.

Sometimes but not often, Crozier and Miss Cracroft found themselves alone, for Jane had endless matters to pursue. Arm in arm, they would stroll the grounds of Government House, she showing him the young groves of oak which as acorns her aunt had carefully stowed in a lacquered box lined with tissue paper on their voyage out.

Peacocks – another of Lady Franklin's extravagant ideas – wandered the lawns, rattling their tails in fantastical iridescent displays, and among the bronze canopy of eucalypts, yellow- and green-winged parrots cut through the air agile as swifts.

One afternoon, Crozier glimpsed half hidden by the rhododendron shrubberies a wallaby raised on its haunches, black tapered paws held close, surveying the couple with cautious indifference, as if they were a distant mirage of the future, and not really there.

The gardens were large and wild and beautiful, the overgrown paths rank with a smell of dead flowers. Dark-stemmed lilies carpeted the ornamental lake across which arched a gold and scarlet bridge painted in the Japanese style.

'Tell me it was a dream, Canot.' Crozier blinks and straightens in his chair. 'Place yourself in those strange parklands, Canot, and stalk our shadows like a ghost.'

'It was a humid day and the grounds teemed with an invisible scurry and chatter of life. Miss Cracroft walked ahead in the cool shade of an avenue of limes towards the rose plantations enclosed by a privet hedge at the centre of which stood a stone bench and a sundial. She picked a sprig of white eglantines and reclined on the seat indicating that I should take my place at her side. She sat in silence for a moment, brow furrowed in thought, the roses wilting on her lap, then turned to me and said:

'"My aunt believes that Sir John has neither the cunning nor the power to deal with persons such as Montagu."

'Was I attentive to her complaint against Franklin's private secretary? Indeed I was not, Canot. Yet I believed she expected me to resist the little moue of her mouth as she uttered Montagu's name, fixing me with stern grey eyes, the colour of English tides.

'Still she went on. "All this hurts Sir John more than you can imagine," she confided. "One thing comes upon another – he takes little exercise, loses in some respect even his appetite, creates imaginary evils, asks my aunt if she can bear if he is recalled in disgrace, and in fact is more agitated and depressed than I have ever seen him."

'How did I reply, Canot? What comfort could I give? Although it occurred to me then that she was speaking out of turn, revealing a side to Franklin that he certainly would not want known, not at least to his Discovery friends.

'"I am sure my uncle is far from well," she continued. "His sensitiveness is beyond conception in this country where people have hearts of stone and frames of iron."

'She bit her lip as if forcing back tears and sent bruised petals scattering from her lap with a fierce sweep of her hand. A frown came between her eyebrows and I longed to smooth it away. Below the bay shone a pure eggshell blue as you might see frescoed in a medieval church beneath a vaulting sky.

'Love-struck fool that I was,' Crozier cries, 'I wanted to hold this young woman in my arms.'

He glances at the miniature oil portrait of Lady Franklin still set above the sideboard, an expression of proud resolution on that once pretty face, as if only *she* could unlock the secrets to the North-West Passage, she seemed to say.

'A vision came to me of a farm nestled in a valley,' Crozier laughs, a sharp bitter bark, 'orchards and vineyards; sheep perhaps grazing lush pastures, hock-high in grass, a simple homestead with a wide veranda overlooking fields of barley and this girl at my side.'

Quietly, I strike a taper to the candles, which an inexplicable draught has extinguished. The sudden flare casts a sulphur tinge like a set of footlights across the commander's hunched form, our hero dragged centre stage, forced to ad lib sage soliloquies in this three-act tragedy of ours.

Let the show go on, the floes scream, flattening hummocks with every exhalation of breath.

'Instead of dreaming, I should have remained rational, calm,' Crozier resumes. 'Enquired further about Sir John Franklin's state of mind, taken down the testimonial of his niece and compiled a fat dossier on the man, which I could have dispatched to the Admiralty on the back of Montagu's damning eye-witness accounts.'

Crozier winces as he peels off his mittens and wrings them dry.

'And had I done so on that day, I can assure you, Canot, we would not be marooned on this ice rink they call King William Land.'

I avert my eyes from the blackened calloused skin.

'Love, Canot,' Crozier whispers, chaffing his palms, 'makes a fool of one.'

I remain silent. Deferential, attentive servant, I remove the empty brandy bottle from the table.

From the passageway, a rasping, scraping sound as if someone in enormous shoes were shuffling by. Crozier lays his mittens to one side and begins to sift through the documents on his desk. He leans forward and selects a quill. At my steady movements about the cabin, he looks up surprised. 'Very well,' he murmurs. 'That will be all, Canot.'

With a gracious bow – *goodnight, sir* – I tiptoe towards the door.

Bedford Square. August 1850.

The Admiralty Board – those lords and political appointees, first and second secretaries – have roused themselves from their torpor and finally referred all operations for the search to the Arctic Council, stout veterans Beechey, Richardson, Ross.

The *Enterprise* and the *Investigator* dispatched under Richard Collinson and Robert McClure, with four more vessels following in their wake, Ross sailing from Scotland in the schooner *Felix*, and a two-ship expedition in the *Lady Franklin* and *Sophia* under Captain William Penny bound for Cape Walker.

Not to be outdone, the Americans have fitted the *Advance* and *Rescue*, financed by the shipping magnate Henry Grinnell, with whom I have pursued an exhilarating and indefatigable correspondence.

And I too triumph in the purchase of my own ninety-ton pilot, the *Albert*, towards which I have committed one thousand guineas of my own private income. Its commander dear Captain Charles Forsyth has taken great heed of my instructions to make for the Great Fish River.

Unable to staunch the flow of public emotion, the Admiralty has finally pledged a ten thousand pound reward for reconnoitring the lost expedition and double that for rescuing the crews. Before long the entire area will be swarming with more ships than any other time in Discovery Service – how can my husband not be found?

Still I must wait out the year's rhythms – winter preparation, spring departure, summer suspense, autumn return.

But I play the part of modern-day Penelope well. Present the public with an unrivalled spectacle of the faithful resolute wife, dressed in funereal black, her dark crêpe and veil mourning absence, not death. People tell me that my resigned and dignified demeanour brings them within the very presence of the lost hero, the tragedy. Only through me, they say, are Sir John Franklin and the plight of his men kept alive.

Even our young Queen is impressed, requesting endless audiences, demanding to be informed at all times of the progress of the ships.

Some might say I would have made a fine actress,

commanding an electrifying silence whenever I enter a room, decorous, loyal, appealing to the protective instincts of admirals, mayors, philanthropists, millionaires, the tenderness of women and their tears recalling the stories of missing men folk, told mother to daughter, sister to sister.

My husband's nephew-in-law rallies to the cause – *Lady Franklin is charming*, Tennyson declares to the world, *so clever yet so gentle and such a lady.*

My dear Alfred, I want to say, I am not so very gentle. I am ruthless.

The grandfather clock chimes nine o'clock. Sighing I lay down my pen – rise stiffly from the chair.

Time to set off to Greenwich for my stepdaughter's wedding, announced without my knowledge or approval yet expecting me to foot the bill. As if I can spare the money or the precious hours.

I glance at my reflection in the looking glass as I reach for my cloak. She will not like me dressed in black. Take my widow's habit as an affront.

I find Sophy waiting downstairs attired in a tulle gown of inoffensive cream, her expression patient, serene.

She is folding another letter to be dispatched by the next departing ship and her devotedness makes me smile sometimes, sweet Sophy my little spaniel pup. In the last missive to Franklin, I found she had written – *you may wonder at my saying that even you do not know your own wife, but in as much as her courage, fortitude and extraordinary mental endowments have never been tested of late, so you have never known the full extent of her rare qualities.*

Lately, however I notice she mentions Crozier in the postscripts – *pray remember me very kindly to Captain Crozier* – and so on, which makes me wonder if she harbours any regrets.

At my approach she looks up and smiles. Over the years, she has lost weight, which accentuates the acute lines of her collarbone, the slightly horsy mouth, yet she had been a beauty once.

Crozier had been nothing but a fool in hoping to court her, illiterate Ulster second-in-command with no prospect of promotion.

Of course we were all seduced, giddied by the sight of the *Erebus* and the *Terror* shouldering their way through the still waters of the Derwent, my husband the first to race down to Sullivan's Cove in rapturous welcome of Captain Ross and Francis Crozier bound for Antarctica, a timely distraction from the petty politicking, the Machiavellian machinations of Government House.

Confined and subjected as one had been to the most intolerable gossip and innuendo, it was quite understandable for Sophy to lose her head, when the bugles called and the church bells rang and all the pretty Hobartian girls tossed posies of violets from the wharf as Crozier and Ross were piped down the gangplank, and escorted with great pomp and ceremony through the narrow streets of our town.

I remember we were blessed that year with a glorious spring, the gorse hedgerows ablaze, wasp-yellow as the diagonal stripes painted across the hull of the Discovery vessels; all our European trees scattering blossom across the paths and the lawns a deep luxuriant green after heavy winter rains. Crozier declared the grounds of Government House a perfect enchantment, and the company of my niece of course.

I do not blame Sophy for any attachment she might have forged in that alien and forsaken place. Van Diemen's Land – senseless penitentiary, ruinous isle of everlasting regret, where I was much maligned and misunderstood despite the best of my intentions. I cherished such dreams. Saw it my destiny to help, improve the destitute, the forsaken, those idle convict women. I believed only I had been blessed with a true vision and under my jurisdiction, could have had it running like a hobby farm. But no one cared, no one would listen. And the more I tried to steer my husband in the right direction, the more we were mocked and most cruelly reviled. Indeed that place broke my heart – I still mourn Mathinna, the native girl I adopted as my own daughter. Should never have listened to the physician who advised the child would not survive an English winter and persuaded me to leave her behind. In my absence, Montagu's cabal exacted their most exquisite punishment. Dispatched Mathinna to an orphanage. Later one of his entourage wrote informing me that the girl had been found drowned in a rivulet, where she had collapsed drunk. How the press had fun with that.

Oh, if I had been born a man – but there's no point now in reflection or self-recrimination.

Suffice to say I made it my duty to dissuade Sophy from such a foolhardy match although she surprised me with her tears, the youthful ardour. Forget Francis Crozier, I said.

Tried to divert her attention instead to the handsome and eminently suitable Captain Ross and in this I succeeded never suspecting he had already pledged his hand to another, unfortunate situation all round.

When we returned to England, Crozier renewed his attentions shortly after his appointment as my husband's second in command. Again Sophy wavered, and again I summoned every argument to ensure his entreaties were repulsed.

Although now I confess there are moments when I wake with a start in the dead of night, chasing a dream which flutters from my mind, and I am weighed with a sense of dread, three in the morning, the suicide hour. I light a candle and reassure myself that I did my best. Gave her sound advice as any mother would to a bewildered child. Taking my place in the dining room, just the two of us – Sophy and me – sometimes I fancy a cold and resentful look flashes across her face, which stops me short and takes away my breath.

I follow Sophy out onto the street where the carriage is waiting. She helps me in, arranging cushions and shawls.

We drive towards the Strand. The Thames runs fast on a rising tide, snakes beneath London Bridge, seeps across the mud flats. A day washed blue with sunlight exactly as Eleanor would have wished for this wedding of hers.

So many ships moored, their halyards slapping, the sound mournful, elegiac like some distant lament. They remind me of my husband's leaving.

The departure of the expedition was meant to be such a triumphant event, the crowds swarming the docks since dawn, the vessels so smartly fitted out.

The handsome young officers assembled in the halls of Admiralty House, Fitzjames, Gore, De Voeux applauding Sir John Franklin, who did his best to rally, afflicted as he was by influenza.

Keenly I had anticipated this moment of good cheer and excitement, everything arranged to perfection – the gaily coloured bunting, the laurel wreaths festooned above trestle tables, a raised dais at one end for speeches, toasts to the Queen. At my own expense I had even hired a photographer to take the portraits of the captains to be published in the press.

Crozier arrived, dishevelled as if he had not slept for weeks, liquor rank on his breath. He pushed past without even a nod or a civil greeting, deliberately turned his back on Sophy and laughed out loud when Fitzjames declared he most fervently hoped they would be frozen in for just one winter.

'So I understand, Captain,' Crozier sneered, 'you and your colleagues have never sailed in Arctic waters.'

What did the man expect and how could he snub his superior like that? After years of Discovery Service, surely he should have known his rightful place by then. Fitzjames remained silent, gave Crozier a generous smile. Franklin looked on distraught. I could not bear to see him affected like this and again I admonished myself for upsetting him the evening before with the unfortunate matter of the flag.

I'm no seamstress but dutifully I embroidered that wretched pennant day and night, Anne's mocking ghost at my side, her disdainful critical daughter obscuring the light from the candle each time she leaned over to inspect my handiwork. Even so, I completed the task, careful not to prick my finger, banishing all thoughts of first wives, of death and blood.

It was late when my husband returned from his final examination of the ships. Hearing his weary tread up the stairs, the laboured breath, I stoked the fire, plumped the cushions on the divan, lit the chafing dish to warm a glass of milk. He came into the parlour, so tired and downcast – *Jane, there is still much to be done* – that I guided him across the room, made him lie down and rest for a while.

When the embers had died in the grate and I heard him snore deep in that troubled chest of his, I gently laid the flag across his knees. I watched his good natured face as he slept – imagined the untold victories he would reap, a trade route to China – when suddenly he woke, tore at the silken cloth in fright and shouted – *Don't you know they lay the Union Jack over a corpse.*

Despite my attempts to soothe him, he remained in an agitated state. All night, I listened to him pace the bedroom next to mine, praying to the Lord.

Watching Crozier drink whisky after whisky in that stifling hall, then pose reluctantly for the photographer – thin-lipped, slit-eyed, drunk – averting his glance from the camera's bright flare, I resolved to make amends with that flag. Send the ships off with a talisman they deserved.

Franklin held me tight – our first real separation – I found myself without words. My mouth dry with a keening sense of desolation. Always I had waved my husband off with such good cheer, knowing that soon we would be reunited, Cairo, Alexandria, Constantinople, Damascus, such cities as you have never seen, and Syria, Egypt, the Holy Land, where I was free to journey on horseback, in the company of a maid, while Franklin served out his Mediterranean peace missions.

I who have sailed the Nile, explored the ancient tombs of Thebes, visited the island of Philae by moonlight and marvelled at the ruins of the Temple of Isis now stood before my husband mute, inconsolable for the first time.

The officers kissed my hand, except Crozier who without a word to anyone had returned to his ship.

I stood on the wharf and fought hard to compose

myself. After all this was our moment of triumph. I had to appear proud and strong before the multitude. The expedition *would* achieve the passage. Faithful Sophy sobbed without restraint despite my offer of a pressed lace handkerchief, Eleanor calling *Papa, Papa,* as Franklin marched onto the poop deck flanked by Fitzjames, Gore, De Voeux. Crozier nowhere to be seen even when a bugle sounded the first note and the cannons were fired. Bad form, I thought.

In the expectant silence that followed, I pointed towards the *Erebus'* mast. 'Why, look,' I cried, 'a dove alighting on the topgallant spars.' The crowd murmured and jostled. 'See,' I shouted. 'A dove, it must be a sign.'

And sure enough, the good people roared and soon set up a resounding chorus – a dove, a dove, heavenly portent, benediction from God – while the officers, my husband included, craned their necks skywards.

On cue, the band began to play – 'Rule, Britannia' – and streamers flew joyously from dock to pier.

How impressionable are the press. Such elated editorials, illustrations even, a dove, angel wings outstretched, flutters among the sails.

Still to this day I am not ashamed. Only I saw fit to orchestrate a miraculous omen at the eleventh hour.

The very thought makes me smile. Sophy glances

across and pats my hand. 'Oh, Jane, you're so brave,' she murmurs.

Yes I am, but not in the way my niece would expect.

It's a long way to Greenwich, and we should have taken a barge, one of those gilt and velvet pleasure cruises so popular among the fashionable in town. I would have preferred the pretty little church in Stanmore where my husband and I were married. But the daughter gave short shrift at that.

'Why, Mama,' Eleanor declared, unable to conceal the undertow of malice in her voice, 'didn't you know it is soon to be demolished?'

So Greenwich it is – the maritime chapel – where Eleanor hopes her father's remains will be returned or failing that a plaque set in his honour.

A bronze plaque to Papa, don't be absurd. Not when I have set my sights on Westminster Abbey.

The carriage rumbles across the cobbled square towards the gates where the clans are waiting, the Gells, the Simpkinsons, attired in all their festive finery, clucking around the groom. At the peeling of bells John Philip Gell, soon to be my son-in-law, hurries inside the church.

The solicitor Sellwood, a florid portly man, who if he saw a chance would cost me a great deal of money, comes forward in breathless greeting. Sophy is led away by some ancient dowager on the Porden side leaving me alone with this man, who Eleanor has employed to spy on the state of my income.

We walk up the path, ancient graves strewn on either side, the marble plinths adorned with figure-heads, ship's wheels, anchors.

'I have received news, madam,' Sellwood begins, 'which will no doubt be of interest.' He darts me a sly glance. 'Concerning your privately financed vessel, the *Albert*.'

I feel my heart quicken and the colour flare to my face. But I manage to meet his gaze pleasantly enough.

'Captain Forsyth intends to turn back, can progress no further.'

He says this only to unnerve me.

'It's too early in the season for such a dispatch,' I reply, coolly, evenly. 'And I have long learned not to believe in rumours.'

'My dear lady, I have it from the highest authority,' Sellwood retorts, driving with each step his ivory-topped cane into the gravel. 'Captain Forsyth met several search vessels at Cape Riley and the information was passed on.'

'To you?' I ask trying to hide the contempt in my voice.

Sellwood gives a self-satisfied nod.

'I make it my business, madam.'

Now he fixes me with a reproachful look.

'Regard it as a blessing, for Captain Forsyth's return will save you an immense expense, which as you know you can little afford.'

Damn the money, I want to exclaim but cannot.

Instead I have to keep pace with this solicitor creeping along the path.

'You will be pleased to hear,' he continues, 'that Forsyth has in his possession several relics discovered at Cape Riley by Captain Erasmus Ommanney.'

Sellwood waves his cane as if conducting a legal inventory.

'Pieces of rope, canvas.'

I listen, abject, hopeful.

'Several animal bones.'

A terrible weariness overcomes me as if I am wading through mud.

'You should take my advice, madam, and leave these matters to the Royal Navy,' Sellwood suggests. 'The professionals.'

We reach the entrance to the church and Sellwood, the gentleman, the gallant, smiles brightly at the filling pews.

'Enough to have squandered your stepdaughter's inheritance on a crank vessel and risked the lives of innocent men,' the lawyer persists. 'Surely even you can see it's of no help to anyone to interfere like this.'

I am guided towards Sophy, prayer book on her lap, gazing dreamily at the mimosa and orchids, the exotic bouquets of hothouse flowers.

Sellwood bows. 'Otherwise, my dear,' he whispers, 'you leave me no choice but to see you in court.'

I take my place beside my niece and clench my hands tight.

Before the altar, the groom stands tall and proud, flanked by one of his clerical cronies who will act as best man.

The organ begins to play and everyone cranes round as Eleanor is led up the aisle by Franklin's cousin, a childhood playmate of hers. She is adorned in the frothing lace of her very own mother's wedding gown, which I consider the height of bad taste. No matter. My opinion on this day will not be required. The maids and pages follow, pretty children I do not recognize. But the matching costumes of velvet and gold brocade must have cost a fortune.

Sophy allows herself to shed a tear or two during the ceremony. I scan the congregation hoping to chance on someone eligible, suitable. But they all seem too young, fidgeting and nudging one another, restless with boredom, eager for the festivities to begin.

Out of habit, I begin to compose a letter to you, Franklin – Mr Gell is now one of the curates of St Martin's and this curacy with one hundred pounds a year from his father and a further fifty pounds as one of the agents for the Propagation of Gospel Society brings him a fixed income to which I add an allowance sufficient to make it up to five hundred a year until the time of your return – I hope if you ever open this note that this news may be of comfort – you may have opened other letters before this – God grant.

Despite myself, I begin to imagine all I could achieve with five hundred pounds – obtain an audience with the President of the United States, refit the *Albert*, stage a charity ball, launch a lottery ticket, offer a substantial reward to the American whalers both in the Atlantic and the Pacific.

But Eleanor and Gell – he now a mere instrument of her indomitable will – stand in my way, obstruct my path. Should Captain Forsyth return with nothing to show than a sack of reindeer bones, they will insist the *Albert* be sold and reap the profits for themselves, lay down the proceeds on some fancy town house – Mayfair, Piccadilly. I shudder at the thought.

The best man proffers the rings. The vows are exchanged. Eleanor throws back her veil and reveals her greatest asset, her mother's glory, lustrous black hair now wreathed in a gleaming plait threaded with silver.

When they kiss, a murmur of approval ripples through the crowd. Eleanor poised and regal as any princess charms all with a beatific smile. How the matrons and dowagers gush, dabbing the corners of their eyes.

If you asked me now, I would freely admit that I have always resented this child, using all her guile to snatch my rightful property, the bills of exchange, which should be mine.

The *Erebus*. 1847.

December – Christmas Eve

Unable to leave the ship on account of the wolves.

A pack of ten has been sighted – gaunt, slouching insatiable beasts, cunning to a degree that confounds all devices for their capture and death. They have taken up residence in a cleft of rock near our vessels and doze for hours out of range but close enough for Fitzjames to observe through a telescope they prick their ears at the slightest noise on deck. 'No one will get within fire of them,' he declared.

Once again the encroaching darkness begins to oppress our fancy. Even the most hard-fisted of boatswains have become jumpy, over-imaginative of late, sighting unaccountable apparitions over the ice plains, sea nymphs, wraiths, lizard-tongued monsters, serpent tails entwined. The usual stuff.

Of most interest on this vessel is the narration of our dreams. Fitzjames told me he was presented to Queen Victoria. Described a gilt ballroom where ladies in satin gowns bobbed and curtsied, blushed behind their ostrich fans, said the tables were spread with every luxury, Egyptian figs, roast partridge, boars steaming on spits, cut crystal decanters brimming with muscatel.

You did well, Canot.

As for me, my dreams remain lustful, sun-drenched, sucking oranges on crescent coves.

Each night, Sirius rises on the meridian from the banked horizon, sometimes oval, hourglass, rhomboid flashing blue and crimson like a revolving light.

We are shabby. Morale is low. Having worn out all our flimsy wardrobes, we've resorted to domestic tailoring. Each day, the officers crochet laddered wool stockings, patch their uniforms, adjust the seat of their breeches. In the mess they gossip and giggle like a Knightsbridge sewing group.

The cold increases. A deep searing pain creeps searchingly from top to toe through to the very marrow of my bones leaving me so stiff that only with effort can I walk on deck and that *limpingly.*

The crew complain of loosening teeth, aching limbs, lethargy.

'Feel like I've taken a good beating,' Fitzjames offers one morning.

Each day I grind molasses hard as granite.

Captain Crozier has retreated to his lair. Although I am summoned to provide liquor, hard stuff, he requests little else and dismisses me with a curt nod. I set the brandy on a butler's tray beside his desk, the latter strewn with charts over which he frets and pores, frantically scratching out every possibility on sheets of paper.

We are phantom pale, servant and master, wax white as a sliced potato. Crozier's eyes have grown large and dark and restless in his head and slide away from mine when I lean forward to ask: *Will that be all, sir?*

Sometimes I gaze at him as if assessing my own reflection in a looking glass, the shocking ghostliness strangely clear.

We have aged, Crozier and I, we feel like old men, our beards tinkling beneath a solid mass of rime. I was staring at him, aghast at the ice-goblins we had become, albino creatures of the night like the vampires you read about in penny novelettes – our fiery breaths steaming with every step – when he peered up at me with a flash of irritation and laid down his pen. The sudden rap of it made me jump.

'May I remind you, Canot,' Crozier murmured, 'we are not baboons.'

He folded his arms and studied me with a thoughtful expression.

'At least, not yet.'

Today, Crozier pulls a face downing his cordial, now a boiled ferment of barley and brown sugar. Looks up startled as if the noxious brew had been my deliberate intent.

Ply him with cheap claret, safest bet.

My steady movements about the room seem to comfort him, the clink of the decanter, the welcoming splash in a tumbler.

'Did I ever tell you, Canot,' Crozier says, 'that when our business in the South was done, I won't bore you with the details,' he shoots me a wry smile, 'we gave a splendid ball here in these ships – this very cabin illuminated with chandeliers.'

From the officers' mess, violins strum a wild refrain to cheers, laughter, the occasional sound of breaking glass.

Covered in canvas, adorned with bunting – sergeants and marines stationed on either side – a dazzling array of yachts formed a continuous bridge to the *Erebus* and

Terror, where the naval officers waited at the entrance to the main decks, the entire lengths of which were ornamented with flags, the Royal Standard proudly hoisted in the centre. Even the hatches had been draped with green and yellow baize, elegant as ottomans in a drawing room.

Around the main mast, a white acacia-fringed canopy served as the supper room and later the quadrille, and gathered on a raised platform at the stern, the band of the 51st Regiment tuned their instruments to the spirit of a stirring waltz. The Royal Crown and the letters V.A. woven in chrysanthemums and marigolds stood at the bows opposite a portrait of the Queen wreathed with sprigs of eucalypt and wild broom. The flicker of hundreds of candles fixed on crossed swords from the spars reflected the most brilliant light, flashing and sparkling in the mirrors arranged all around the vessels' sides.

'There was not the least vestige,' Crozier murmurs, examining his frost-bitten hands, 'to indicate that the visitors were shipboard, except of course the decks.'

A fragrance of lily of the valley heralded the young ladies of Hobart Town. How they giggled and whispered and teetered in satin slippers towards the handsome officers at the rail. All wore light silk variations in blue to compliment their hosts – one girl exclaiming as she blushed before Captain Ross that it was her sole desire to go to sea with the ships. At this, dapper, fearless Ross conducted his swooning charge to the great stern cabin, transformed into tasteful apartments so that the gentler sex could pin posies to their décolletage then the very height of fashion.

Accompanied by Sir John Franklin, Sophy Cracroft made her way along the gangplank to a fanfare of trumpets and whistles, cutting an elegant figure in ivory and cream, no frivolous blooms adorned those braids pulled tight at the temples.

Crozier thrilled to see the niece, grown thinner since the expedition south, which had chipped five hard months from his life, yet a smile of recognition hovered at her lips when quickly he stepped forward and politely enquired as to her aunt. No surprise to hear that Jane Franklin was scaling mountain peaks in New Zealand – why attend a mere ball when there were so many first summits to score.

Instead a lightness buoyed Crozier's heart as he ushered Miss Cracroft to the refectory where the captain's stewards furnished the necessary essentials of lemonade and cold punch. Sir John Franklin, he noticed, was making a sterling effort among the crowd, engaged in dutiful conversation although a tremor ran down his left side each time he stooped and bowed.

'Dreadful row with Montagu,' the niece whispered following his gaze. 'I doubt he shall recover from it. The man means to kill him, I am sure.' As she talked, Crozier allowed himself to admire her severe beauty, pearls twined around the long slender neck, the determined set of her mouth in that oval face. Fixing him with a faint look of reproach, she informed him that Sir John would never be happier than at the helm of a discovery ship.

'Why, my aunt overheard Montagu declare that he would sweat Sir John as long as he lived. If only Uncle were given another command.'

All around them, ceaseless gossip and merriment.

Hemmed in by the eager damsels of Hobart Town, Captain Ross held court. The good ladies clamoured to know how many times during the London season he had seen the Queen and was she very pretty?

One bold country girl pressed forward and confided in a loud whisper that when the Governor first arrived Lady Franklin had invited them to an evening party which had been keenly anticipated yet they had found themselves stuck in a room full of pictures and books and shells and stones and other rubbish, with nothing to do but hear people talk lectures or sit mute as mice listening to what was called good music. Her voice rose with indignation.

'Why could not Lady Franklin have had the military band in, and the carpets out, and given dances, instead of such stupid preaching about philosophy and science, and a parcel of stuff nobody could understand?'

At this, Captain Ross threw back his head and laughed. And overhearing, Crozier too suppressed a smile.

The niece showed her disapproval by clicking open her fan, not before Crozier noticed she darted Ross a quick appraising glance.

'I understand Captain Ross is a man of much influence in the Admiralty,' she enquired, allowing Crozier to lead her to the first dance.

'Indeed,' he replied, aware of a catch in his throat as he placed his palm against hers. 'With Sir John Barrow in particular, whose zeal has done much to expand the Queen's Empire.'

The young girl moved elegantly back and forth and, as the music quickened, lost some of her stiff reserve, the corseted upright stance that reminded Crozier of the aunt. And he too surprised her with his agility and grace, this bluff seaman guiding their step through the throng, which gathered and swung away again until it was time to exchange partners in the next round. With a pang, Crozier noted the niece now curtsied before Captain Ross, who clasped her wrists with an expression of boyish expectation. Crozier found himself with the country girl. She thundered towards him and fairly wrenched his arms from their sockets at every twirl.

Watching Ross and Miss Cracroft in perfect rhythm, Crozier was struck by how well suited they seemed, quite a couple, he of aquiline nose and chisel jaw, and she leaning her head prettily against one broad shoulder – the two of them weaving so easily across the floor as if for years they had been dancing like this at a ball. The plump freckled cleavage of Crozier's girl panted and heaved, a clump of peonies flapped from her décolletage. There was no mistaking the ardour in that bold stare. A yeast smell of sweat rose sharp and when she flashed him a smile, her teeth were white and even.

The niece's gown swished his legs as she glided past, still partnered with Ross. Crozier thought he could endure no more.

'Perhaps it was the mimosa, Canot,' Crozier murmurs beneath his breath. 'Heady and pungent that giddied my senses on that evening of the ball.'

A desultory chime of six bells rings from the deck. No one pays heed to shipboard time any more – the twilight stretch of hours much the same to us now.

Watching them, Crozier confides, he could admire the niece anew, from a tantalizing distance, Ross steering her through the crowd. He bore no grudge against his captain, who earlier had confided that he had pledged his soul to another, and from the moment he set foot on British soil, would refuse all offers of a next command.

Instead Ross displayed the niece before his hungry eyes and Crozier saluted him as they whirled by.

At last, with a flourish, the musicians set down their instruments and bowed. The dancers bumped to a sudden halt and began to hurry along the deck, the red-haired country girl leading the way, calling for refreshments and chilled glasses of hock.

Crozier found Miss Cracroft alone at the ship's bows leaning against the rail. Ross had been summoned to join Sir John's circle.

The commander reaches out in the darkness as if he feared his servant might have slipped out unnoticed and he would find himself alone.

'How can I describe the change in the niece,' he resumes, 'her animated face, framed by a cloud of curls springing loose from her braids.

'At my approach, she turned to me with an expression of immense gratitude: "Captain Ross has assured Sir John of an expedition," she said. "He will petition the Admiralty the moment his vessels dock at Deptford. I can't wait to tell my aunt."

'We stood close, our shoulders almost brushing.

' "Francis," she whispered, "if I may be so bold to call you so, I will pray morning and night for your safe passage home."

' "My darling girl," I murmured. "Marry me, Miss Cracroft."

'There, the words so fiercely rehearsed were out.'

Crozier grimaces, his mouth stained with wine.

The band has reassembled, cane chairs creak as the musicians take their place with a whining rasp of instruments tuned.

'The niece flushed,' Crozier continues. 'Her lips parted – and from the supper room I could hear Ross propose the first bumper to the health of our Queen – I willed Miss Cracroft to release me with one simple *yes* from a decade of servitude; unbearable solitude, more keenly felt with each passing year than the most wretched of castaways.

'With a start she came to as if awakened from a trance. "No," she cried and snatched away her hand. "It is James, I mean Captain Ross, whom I love." '

Crozier lets out a sigh, which turns to a cough.

'Sometimes on service it can take five years,' he says in a toneless voice, 'for the canker to eat away at your soul, to destroy some part of you, sometimes it happens in the first few months. That is when the rage comes. And when people become murderous.'

He glances my way. 'But you know this, of course. The little fool,' he whispers.

Behind him the portrait of Lady Franklin looks down with that knowing patrician smile.

After the old gentleman's death, no one, not even Crozier, could bring himself to remove the miniature from where it hung above the sideboard. And not once, throughout the ice-artillery bombarding our vessels, has it fallen. There Lady Franklin will remain, glazed mosaic for all eternity, for centuries to come.

Bedford Square. April 1851.

Spring comes, wet, stormy sending flurries of leaves scurrying across the square.

My vessel, the *Albert*, is back, having penetrated no further than seventy miles into Prince Regent Islet. Forsyth had the audacity to present himself personally to my rooms, carrying the piteous relics, scraps of rope and sailcloth in a round wicker basket adorned with white paper like a twelfth-night cake.

Bitterly he complained that his ice-masters were untrustworthy, boorish, who differed as widely as the Poles on the correct route and the American clerk, William Parker Snow, self-inflated, impossible and of no service at all.

Strutting back and forth, declaiming wildly, Forsyth proved a grievous disappointment.

His expedition had accomplished nothing. Still it brought news of further discoveries on Beechey Island

– those bleak headlands of Wellington Channel I had always wanted examined, and which now must be followed up. On that resolution, public opinion is united, supported in the Commons by Richard Cobden, Benjamin Disraeli and Sydney Herbert.

And I have two suitors pressing for the cause – a new commander in William Kennedy, former fur trader, half Orkneyman, half Cree, who having lived eight years among the Innu of Labrador can handle both kayak and sledge. He wrote stating he had little nautical experience nor was he the stuff of which leaders are made yet was willing to sail and act as a subordinate to anyone in view we would prefer.

So now I pour tea in the Nagasaki porcelain for the Canadian's second in command, twenty-five-year-old Enseigne de Vaisseau Joseph-René Bellot, who reclines elegantly on the ottoman before me. Nothing can animate a woman of my age more than this impeccable diminutive Frenchman with dark expressive eyes and pouting cherubic lips, attesting in a clear voice that he would readily jeopardize his career in the marine to devote himself to the Search.

'Trust me, Lady Franklin,' Bellot takes the cup I proffer in his delicate childlike hands, 'I have a good star which does not forsake me.'

How I enjoy conversing in the courtly language of romance, although his English is perfectly fluent.

'Your conduct, madam,' he says, 'is regarded without example in the annals of conjugal piety and does honour to a whole epoch and an entire nation.'

Nicely put. I reward him with a platter of Sophy's shortbread.

'A Frenchman participating in such an enterprise,' he continues, 'should be seen as the first application of the grand ideas of international union as displayed by the Great Exhibition.'

We look at one another with mutual admiration.

Taking a fastidious bite from his biscuit, Bellot informs me he has gone to considerable lengths to accustom his body to the cold and made himself sleep an entire winter without a single blanket – he feels the intrepidity of his heart requires conflict, the activity of his imagination the spectacle of grand scenes of nature and for the satisfaction of all his faculties he must journey through new and unknown countries.

'I have always enjoyed a facility in understanding and speaking all languages,' he confides. 'I do not know Russian but will learn it on this expedition so as to communicate with the whalers.'

I confess I am beginning to fall a little in love with this man. Shame he is far too young for Sophy.

When I enquire into the details of his kit and equipment, he shrugs and shakes his head.

'Well then, I shall supply your mother's place and provide a warm suit of clothes,' I declare. 'And when the *Albert* sets sail, the French flag will be raised in your honour.'

'Ah, madam,' Bellot cries, 'if only you could read my heart to see how swiftly the somewhat egotistical desire of making an extraordinary voyage has been succeeded by a real ardour and a genuine passion for the end we aim at. If you take the place of my mother, well then, I will be to you a son.'

He leans forward and grasps my hand, pressing my bony knuckles against his cheek in a charming gesture of filial devotion.

Such chivalry I have not witnessed in a long time.

'Come now, monsieur,' I say to lighten the mood, 'your character might be sad and thoughtful yet I believe your spirit is gay.'

I am graced with a radiant smile.

'Oh yes,' he replies. 'I am not a drawing-room man, go out little in society, yet dancing is the only pleasure of which I am passionately fond.'

'Good, for I will enjoy watching you lead the good ladies of Stromness in energetic rounds of the Schöttische, my dearest French son.'

When with elaborate bows and farewells, the enthusiastic Bellot takes his leave; I find myself foolishly aflutter and seek Sophy downstairs in the parlour to soothe such unseemly agitation in a woman of my years.

She sits at the table by the window, dipping a quill in ink, absorbed in her letters. Not Crozier again.

At my approach, she glances round with an eager expression.

'A supporter to our cause has bequeathed seven carrier pigeons and has been experimenting with different chemicals to find the best method of marking them.'

There's a cooing sound at my niece's feet. Looking down, I espy a wicker cage draped with her best emerald travelling shawl.

'To keep them quiet,' Sophy explains. 'Although they've had plenty of wheat.'

So I can see from the scatterings of husks on the carpet.

'Netty says she'll take them to her brother's place until the *Albert* sets sail. He's quite an expert and will keep them in good shape.'

Sorting through the papers, Sophy begins to expand on her plan – a cross on the breast either in black or red ink to be used only in the event of good news – not necessarily implying the safety of Sir John Franklin –

here she frowns – but that the missing Expedition has been found.

Drawing back the shawl, she raises the lid of the coop and with a swift determined movement, seizes a bird, which, secured in her hands, settles on her lap.

'Lady Ross, the champion,' Sophy explains, stroking the snow-white plumage, 'to be sent only under the joyful circumstance of Sir John's individual rescue and safety.'

The creature surveys me with bright beady eyes. I imagine her soaring high above the *Albert*'s sails, ice-rings around her throat, her own breath rimed against her breast on the perilous pilgrimage home.

With all my heart I wish brave Lady Ross well.

I tell Sophy that I've booked a passage to Aberdeen on a steamer to oversee the refitting of the ship.

She darts me a reproachful look.

'We can't afford the train,' I say, 'costs having run high and subscriptions lower than expected with all England distracted with the Crystal Palace exhibition.'

Sophy gives a dutiful nod. 'Of course not,' she says managing a smile although we both know she'll be sick all the way.

Wretched journey – I will not subject my niece to that again – and Aberdeen one incessant whirl, revising orders, agreements, allotments, the ship's articles. Whenever we visit the *Albert*, a crowd gathers and follows us along Union Street to our shabby lodgings, cramped rooms, worn linen, bedbugs in the mattresses, although I should not complain, for our proprietor recognized me at once and offered us full board gratis.

Today, the patient onlookers waiting on the wharf are rewarded as they watch the ornate mahogany and gilt organ generously donated by the Prince Consort hoisted aboard, its monstrous jet-black legs bumping against the rail. *Keep her steady*, the crew call. Anxiously viewing the proceedings through the stern window of the captain's cabin, I wonder if smaller instruments would have made more sense on such a tightly packed vessel, violins for a string quartet perhaps.

'The ice scenes have again recommenced,' declares a voice. I turn round and there's William Coppin, arms outstretched in greeting at the doorway.

'My dear departed daughter Weesy remains adamant that the search should be directed towards Prince Regent's Inlet. And so it shall, my lady.'

Coppin's visits cheer me, and he has remained true to his word in taking charge of all expedition finances. How this upright gentleman reassures, dismisses my apprehensions, his manner patriarchal, benevolent, sound money too in the expensive tailored suits, silk shirts and cravats, the elegant whalebone cane held in one gloved hand. So calm and capable is this resolute shipbuilder, understanding at once all that needs to be done.

'Why, it's a Leviathan,' I say pointing towards the organ swinging and straining against the ropes. 'I don't suppose we could find a tactful way of leaving it behind.'

Coppin sadly shakes his head. 'Nuisance, all round. Clearly the Prince Consort is not nautically inclined.'

There's a cheer from the crowd when the colossus is finally lowered onto the starboard side.

'I have just left Monsieur Bellot at his lodgings,' Coppin declares, 'detained him with a French newspaper so I could make the necessary arrangements.'

Again I admire his calm, purposeful demeanour.

'I've taken the measure of the ship,' he says, 'and with Captain Kennedy's agreement and the help of a carpenter, it's a matter of removing several shelves to transform the butler's pantry into suitable quarters for our gallant first officer.'

He slaps fifteen guineas on the table between us – which I match from my own purse. Then he proffers a further five to furnish Bellot with books he might require on the long voyage out.

'Decent fellow,' he murmurs. 'Become quite fond of him. He will do you proud, Lady Franklin.'

How Bellot thrills at his brand-new kit, the double-lined wool uniform, the gold-braided officer's cap, his trunk filled with polar narratives, the works of Shakespeare and Byron, his own quarters freshly varnished and painted.

'Why, madam,' he exclaims, 'I did not expect such attention.'

We are all gathered in the captain's great stern cabin, waiting for propitious winds to speed us to Stromness.

Sophy, who even feels queasy when the *Albert* is moored, presses a handkerchief to her lips.

Before the toasts, Bellot makes a fine speech – I find in Lady Franklin a heart which comprehended mine at once, and an affinity which established itself between two souls – the soul of a rare woman who has elevated to heroism the accomplishment of great duty, of a wife who devotes her fortune and her whole life to the search for her husband – and the soul of a young officer, her French son, Joseph-René Bellot.

When the fifteen-strong Shetlander crew come aboard, Captain Kennedy pronounces the *Albert* a temperance ship sailing under cold-water colours.

Only I register the look of alarm on Bellot's face.

'I fear an absence of wine,' he confides, 'might make

my digestion difficult. Yet for a man of resolution, what else is the body than a slave that must obey and what are physical wants but habit?'

He smiles.

'No doubt this precaution will give an unprecedented lustre to our expedition.'

I shall miss Bellot and long to accompany him on the mission.

The ship's organ plays 'The Girls We Left Behind' as the *Albert* ploughs high running seas. Were it not for the first officer's steady guidance, our impetuous Captain Kennedy would certainly have lost the jib-boom by carrying too much sail.

When the island of Ramsay looms before us, I join Bellot on deck.

'Nothing can be wilder than this scene,' he calls through the wind, gesturing towards the perpendicular basalt cliffs, the headlands covered in a rugged red mantle of heath. 'At last,' he cries, 'I have reached the summit of my wishes, happier and more favoured by circumstance than I could ever have ventured to hope.'

'And what will you call your future discoveries?' I ask.

'After those dear to my country,' he solemnly replies, 'and especially the names of those to whom I owe much gratitude.'

He turns and gazes at me with such an expression of youthful ardour that to my astonishment, tears prick my eyes.

I point out the harbour of Stromness, always a pretty place, the steep cobbled whitewashed streets, the gaily painted fishing boats listing on their moorings and such a crowd to greet us, many of the islanders still remembering my husband's departure on his first Arctic mission in 1819.

Dressed, rested, refreshed – Sophy remains confined to her bed after her ordeal of mal de mer – I take my place next to the formidable Mrs Rae, the Hudson Bay traveller's mother, in the illuminated village hall where Bellot dances reel after Scottish reel with the young damsels of the town. Now he guides Mrs Rae's niece across the floor. Admiring his elegant supple form, I find myself blushing, stupid creature that I am.

Mrs Rae leans against my chair and informs me it has been a while since she has received word from her John. There is something unsettling about this old woman's presence which I can't quite explain. Indeed she is beautiful, the white braids coiled at the nape of her neck, the piercing blue eyes fixing me now and then with a sharp knowing look. When I confide I had written expressing my utmost confidence in her son's ability to do what few other men could accomplish in the quest for my husband, she purses her mouth in a thin mocking line as if John Rae were destined for more noble pursuits than tracking a buffoon of an English commander trapped on the ice. Her very stance, the proud straight back, the way she surveys the room, the imperial nod if she sees someone she recognizes, seem to diminish me in some imperceptible way. In short, Mrs Rae makes me feel a fool.

I see Bellot has her niece quite out of puff, and the shine to her complexion is most unbecoming. He advances through the throng towards us and gives Mrs Rae a courtly bow. She scrutinizes him up and down.

'You are able to converse with Mr Kennedy in his native tongue,' she asks in that soft lilting brogue of hers.

'Why yes, Mr Kennedy speaks Canadian French,' Bellot declares. 'That is to say the French of more than a century ago, and I am glad to hear from time to time some of those old expressions which have a perfume quite peculiar to themselves.'

His reply appears to please her for she smiles.

'I charge you with all my affectionate remembrance should you meet John.'

Rising to her feet, Mrs Rae strides across the room

and joins her niece at the oak trestle table where refreshments are being served.

Bellot glances after her. 'If the woman be such a man, what must the son be?'

And he laughs.

'I confess,' Bellot whispers, 'that I am not insensible to the charms of these young beauties, that Miss H, the white lily, and Miss R, the brilliant rose, have not counted for nothing in the pleasures of this evening. Except—'

He sits down beside me with a sigh.

'Sometimes I'm afraid the smallness of my stature makes me too much marked in a quadrille.'

'Nonsense,' I retort.

Drear dawn, a dull grey glint on the horizon – we gather on the wharf, the timbers dark and gleaming, the colour of mussel shells. One by one the Admiralty flags are hoisted. The men mustered. The cannon saluting from the docks find their answer in the ship's mortar.

Bellot clasps my hands.

'Trust in the inexhaustible devotion of a son, who goes in search of his father,' he murmurs, 'and what human strength can, I will do.'

Take care of yourself, is all I can manage to say.

All too soon, the word is given, the hawsers passed and the steam tug takes the *Albert* in tow. How small and frail the vessel seems, buffeted by wild rushing currents.

Despite a chilling rain misting the sky, I refuse to move until the ship's sails disappear behind the lone rocky sentinel of the Old Man of Hoy.

The *Erebus*. 1848.

January – month of oysters and stout

Desire for fresh meat drives us like a disease.

To shoot a seal, practise the Esquimaux tactics of endurance and immobility. All day I wait, my ancient carbine branding my hands. One by one, the seals rise breast-high from their water-holes, treading water with their tails, only to dip again at my rasping breath.

Take aim. Fire.

The ball does not kill outright. Blood oozes from its snout. The creature looks at me with an expression of startled reproach, dips again, comes up, thrashes flurriedly and sinks once more. Lost.

I shoot another and roll its packed body over the drift plains. Back in the galley, I find one toe frostbitten, tallow-looking, dead flesh. Restore by snow rubbing. Serves me right.

Outside, beneath moon shadows, the crew play football. A bear thunders across the ice, takes off with the ball.

Our world has shrunk to Lilliput. We creep like rats into every crevice and crack, scavenge the warped planks. Find a warm corner, where we gather into ourselves for a brief moment of silence. Numb and cold, not daring to remove our boots, we retreat into the furthest recesses of the hull – furled tight like creatures unborn yearning for warmth.

Above all, we have begun to fear ourselves and keep to worn solitary tracks burrowing deeper into the darkness.

Sirius our fickle sun and everywhere a smell of the grave and the shroud.

We crave colour, for the Dog Star to flash blue then crimson.

Eagerly my mind fastens like a leech on mackerel skies, long evenings of meadow grass and lark song.

And the welter of irritation stirred by the most trivial offence; the whinnying whistle of a man's snore; the indolent swing of someone's legs against the bulkheads above your hammock; or the ice-master's penchant for Negro melodies breaking out from time to time, with scraps of 'I'm off to Charleston, a little while to stay'.

At least his tuneless warbles bring a smile to Coffin's thin anxious face.

Not to mention the rattle of my own pots and pans in the galley, coaxing the monstrous yaw of the stove, the murmured protests from the men ranged head to foot on the orlop deck; *Christ's sake, lay it off, damn you, Canot.*

Huddled beneath furs in the library, as a flame glows and gusts on its blackened wick, the candles now rationed to one hour in an endless night, I have squandered my entire share on *Robinson Crusoe* – ah for a tropical isle on which to build an empire of driftwood and salvaged rope – yet unable to reach the end of the narrative before *lights out*. Extinguished in a pinprick, a single spark, no larger than a diamond stud fastening a gentleman's cravat.

All around, a scamper and rustle, teeth gnawing through timber. I have seen some of the men catch vermin with their bare hands and devour them raw. The officers begin to dread the sight of their blood-frozen faces.

But for now I am blind, unable to read the book on my lap. Will have to grope my way out, clasp the tasselled curtain cords, which I have knotted from the chair to the door for this very purpose. I stare into the shimmying shadow layers, hoping to catch their ebb and flow, a glimpse of shelf-lined walls, the shaft of a lit taper sliding along the threshold. Then I could call out – wait, sir, and I will follow.

This evening, which could be dawn, morning or noon, the ship seems strangely quiet. I strain to listen. Low rumblings around the bows, dull vibrations somewhere aft, the infernal ship's bell ringing to no purpose day and night.

When I was a child, I remember a nurse who hummed Breton songs to lull me to sleep, strange haunting lullabies of shipwrecks and mariners lost at sea. Outside the waves would splinter against the rocks; gale-swept spume flecking my attic window in filigrees of salt, as if the breath of some beast had rimed each pane with the rough rasp of its tongue. Hush, my nurse would whisper, if wide-eyed I tossed and turned. And she would ask me to imagine black velvet draping the ceilings and wood-panelled walls, muffling the door, my sheets and pillows downed with smooth fur, cocooning and safeguarding me against the perils of the night, the remorseless rake of the tides. Again she would sing to me in her low-throated peasant voice and I would succumb to the dreamless slumber of the infant I once was.

Sometimes, but not often, sitting here fearful and

alone, plunged into a darkness unimaginable to anyone at home, without even the patterned constellations for comfort, Sirius, mere ghost, troubled mirage trembling the skies, I am tempted to stride out on deck in slippers and nightshirt; rail the empty heavens to turn my heart to flint, tears to stone. Allegorize myself as a rock, held firm on some strait or bay in Arctic seas still and at peace beneath the quiet shine of the moon's eclipse Yet—

Poor Crozier looks very bad. Has grown tall and thin, long toothed with the yellow fangs of a wolf – his deerskin gloves are monstrously large and it is pitiful to see him striving once again to gnaw the abandoned soup bones for scraps of meat.

Most days he orders me to inventory the stores – and steeling myself I venture into those echoing crypts. Dread drawing the bolt from the door and stepping into the drizzle of condensation dripping from the walls. Sometimes I disturb Coffin crouched on a pile of hessian he has dragged into a narrow cubicle between the bread bins, and blinking he raises one arm in fright against the sudden flare of torch light.

Only yesterday he flew into one of his manias, declared he still clearly remembered how I had threatened him with a revolver and assured me that he would steal the march next time, *oh yes mark his words, he will*, and would try to kill me the moment he saw we might not make it home.

This morning, tiptoeing inside, I glimpse his shadow gliding behind the tea chests from Ceylon. If he approaches me, I shall say nothing.

I wish Osmer were at my side, notebook and pencil in hand: two months of tinned provisions – three shelves of rancid ox stew and bully beef, six barrels of salt fish, which the crew detest, and thirty containers of flour, oats, barley, lard and hard tack. *However we have tobacco and grog in plenty*, I can hear Osmer announce in a triumphant tone.

It's the dwindling supplies of fuel which bother us the most. Those fit enough to work have begun cannibalizing the ship, starting with the beams in the gunroom.

Rations, per regulation, have been reduced for each man by a third, I inform Crozier. To husband our coal reserves, all meals except for one a day are eaten cold, and the lower deck heated sparingly during the darkest hours.

Spring, Crozier endlessly mutters beneath his breath, *abandon the ships and march to the Great Fish River.* When he talks like this, I try to cheer him with the last of the fine brandies, several cases donated to the expedition by the good citizens of Stromness.

Lady Franklin still fixes him with that inscrutable gaze. Sometimes when I move about the room her portrait gives me an uneasy feeling, as if something unfriendly were watching the back of my neck.

Spring. How we pray for that same summer garish burst on Beechey Island, moss green as any English garden splashed blue and purple with saxifrage, cranberry and harebell.

Again I think of Franklin – of the feast I prepared at the end of May eight months ago when we wearied of waiting for leads to appear on these shores. Word ran round the ship that our captain had an important announcement to make.

I am often haunted by this vision of myself – Canot the cook and Osmer fretting when I handed him the list of supplies – *Tinned lobster, duck, quail*, he enquired, *surely these should be saved for a more festive time?*

I shrugged. Franklin's orders, I said, past caring. I was tired. My feet ached as if I were stepping on shards of glass each time I marched from the glacial storerooms to the furnace of the galley, freeze and thaw, my stockings either creaking with ice or wet through, slush soaking the soles of my boots. Coffin too limped at my side, wheeling the trolley.

'What can it mean, Canot?' Osmer asked studying the shelves. 'Something we've not been told?'

A smile spread across Coffin's wizened sun-starved face.

I did not want to discourage the boy.

'Perhaps,' I said, stacking the provisions one by one.

Back in the galley, Coffin fairly skipped from cauldron to saucepan, stirring wine in the stock, one hand clenched around the spoon, his fingers swollen purple as ripe plums.

'Are we going home, sir?'

'I don't know, Coffin,' I murmured. 'Let us hope so.'

The ship hushed when we clattered towards the captain's cabin as if everyone were waiting for instructions to turn the vessels about, full steam ahead, and quick about it. Except the propellers had been unshipped for almost a year now.

We found the officers at their designated places; Franklin stationed at the head the table. Crozier not invited, I noticed.

Franklin distributed a set of charts to his men. 'I intend to send out a reconnaissance,' he announced, 'to search for any sign of open channels beyond the vantage of the lookouts.'

Fitzjames leaned forward, eager, expectant.

'The expedition will proceed south-east,' Franklin

began, 'and cache ashore a cylinder in the cairn built seventeen years ago by Captain Ross at Victory Point between the headlands he kindly named Cape Jane Franklin and Franklin Point.'

He gestured towards Coffin to pour the wines. I lit the chafing dish and arranged the duck breasts on a platter.

'We will not report that our ships are beset,' Franklin continued. 'But wintered in the ice, on Beechey Island, 1845–1846, Sir John Franklin commanding – all well.'

Franklin raised a glass of water to his men.

'No cause for alarm. The coming summer will soon release us.'

Fitzjames was the first to lead the cheers – All's well.

Coffin was kept busy with the claret as the officers downed their share in greedy gulps.

Standing beside them, you could feel the tingle of their anticipation – action at last, scour every inch of the ice litter for promising straits; discover the North-West Passage perhaps.

'It is my intention that Mr Gore and Mr De Voeux will lead the party in the company of six able seamen,' Franklin declared. 'And fix our position at a latitude of 70-05 north and longitude 98-23 degrees west.'

Fitzjames choked on his wine.

Gore flushed and straightened in his chair.

'Mr Gore,' Franklin resumed, 'you will enclose in the report a brief account of our mission since our departure from England.'

The lieutenant sat bolt upright, all brisk attention. Would have saluted had he not been at the table.

'Yes, sir.'

'And I dare say,' Franklin paused and studied his papers, 'we need not mention the three unfortunates who perished on Beechey Island.'

'No, sir.'

Franklin's instructions set Osmer in a tizz. How he fussed, sorting the warmest slop clothing, flannel underwear, woollen drawers, blue cloth trousers, red worsted shirts, heavy outer frock coats of strong twill, Welsh wigs and watch caps, comforters, fox-fur mittens, stout leather shoes cleated for ice work and thigh-high waterproof canvas fishermen's boots.

'Not forgetting,' he muttered, rummaging through the chests, 'sixteen pairs of wire-mesh goggles.' These unwieldy contraptions he held up for me to view. 'To prevent snow blindness,' he announced as if I didn't know.

The expedition was issued a brown Holland tent,

eight wolf-skin robes, twenty-four Hudson Bay Company blankets, additional towing lines, two shotguns and an axe.

I had to rustle one week's worth of provisions – pemmican, ship's biscuit, fifty pounds of tinned provisions, Goldner's best, soups and meats they could scour from a can. I assembled the cooking kits – frying pans, spirit stoves, cotton-wicked lamps, bottles of ether stowed in wicker baskets.

At dawn, Gore directed his crew to strap their harnesses and secure the ropes. The sledge piled improbably high, its silk pennant emblazoned with the name of our Queen.

The men could barely move, elephantine, swaddled tight as newborns in their gear. From the decks, we watched them stagger and slip hauling their load. Unrecognizable in helmets, goggles and gloves, they looked up at us to a peal of trumpets. We cheered them, these creatures from another planet tunnelling a voyage to the centre of the earth.

For a long time, we charted their creeping progress, black specks trekking purposefully across a grey plain that met the unearthly blood glow of the horizon. Onwards they trudged in caterpillar formation towards ridges and valleys packed hard as flint, beneath still cloudless skies and a cutting north wind on their backs.

We imagined we could hear the crunch of their boots against the terrible wastes of snow, the tinkle of their breath.

For hours we stood on deck blinking into the dazing radiance trying to trace their shadows, until our eyes blistered and our lashes froze.

The following day and the day after that, time itself vanished in an eternity of waiting. Entire years elapsed between the ringing of the bells, minutes stretched into hours, even the busy tick of the chronometers slowed.

And the ice eerily silent, a steady monotonous creaking, signifying nothing – no change – for the seasons had fled.

Fitzjames and his remaining officers gathered in the mess room, engaged in futile calculations as to the exact distance the men might have travelled so far; should a blizzard fall, would they manage on the stores? And of course they circled the question, which preyed on us all – the possibility that they might not return.

A week passed. At dawn, a shout from the crow's nest, Gore and De Voeux half carried, half dragged to the ships by six topmen. The crew raced down and helped them aboard. Sir John Franklin waited on the poop, hands clasped in prayer.

The officers unrecognizable, encased with ice, skin cankered and mottled in a blank featureless face, their very nostrils, eyelids, even their blackened tongues scalded by the sun. The men had fared no better; they stood trembling, frost-bitten and burnt in turn.

Goodsir the surgeon summoned at once. I was dispatched to the galley. Boil kettles and quick about it. At my command, Coffin obeyed every order, raking the embers, pulling at the pumps. We loaded the trolley and clanked our way to the sick bay.

What a sight. Oblivious to the agonized cries of his charge, Goodsir unpeeled the heel of a stocking with a pair of tweezers from a welter of swollen flesh. And the stench that filled the room had Coffin retching.

The officers hovered by the door and watched Goodsir wrap the men in warm flannels, place hot-water bottles beneath their arms and on their chests. Franklin paced up and down, willing one of them to wake from their delirium and report the sighting of leads at once.

Towards early afternoon as a violet twilight leached from the skies, Gore half-opened one bruised eye. Franklin kneeled before him. It was dreadful to see the old gent crouched over the youth like that, praying for him to speak as if he had one ear clamped at the confessional, straddling a chasm between redemption and damnation.

Goodsir held a cup to the charred lips. Gore managed a shaky sip. Brandy splashed his chin. Franklin leaned close, reached out to steady the anguished lolling head.

For an hour, we waited in that close, fetid cabin, Goodsir and I, piling eiderdowns and blankets on each stricken form, swabbing wounds, trying to decipher the moans whispered from soaked sheets.

'Captain,' Gore finally murmured. The strangled voice stopped everyone in their tracks. Goodsir quietly set down a spittoon on the tray I was carrying. We tiptoed towards the narrow trestle bed. Franklin rested on his heels, breathing heavily.

'Captain,' Gore said again. A tear brimmed the one good eye and coursed down his cheek, 'travelling in this country is very discouraging.'

With effort, Franklin rose to his feet.

'Nothing then?'

'No, sir.'

Coffin sobbed, the racking, desolate weeping of an inconsolable child.

Slowly Sir John turned to his officers.

'Muster the crews.'

Our captain climbed unsteadily onto the quarter-deck like the old man he was.

His cloak flew out in a sudden gale and he had to shout to make himself heard.

'There will be no 1847 release, no voyaging this summer, no crack at the Passage. For that, we will have to endure another year.'

Fitzjames stood firm beside him and surveyed the men. Not a murmur from the waist, as if they had known all along. Crozier stared straight ahead, no emotion betrayed on that sallow face.

The crews listened with an unnerving stoic silence.

'Brave souls,' Franklin cried. 'We will over-winter and be on our way next season, straight through to China. In the meantime, the rum and tobacco issue will continue at full allowance.'

This at least roused ragged cheers from the wretches confined to the orlop deck. That night officer Gore died in the sick bay – strong, young, so rapidly undone by his excursion into the ice plains.

From then on, the Old Gentleman confined himself to his cabin, sat head turned to the wall, gazing into nowhere, telescope propped like a carbine across his knees, defeat and resignation furrowing his brow.

Despite the paunch, the general impression of corpulence, of having gone to seed, he left his meals untouched. Not a crumb.

Five days after the return of the defeated expedition, it was Goodsir who discovered Franklin dressed in full uniform, the polished medals pinned beneath his left shoulder. His features puffy, pallid, the lips pursed as they had been in life.

He sat staring at the miniature of his wife.

No sign of a struggle in the ordered room, the grandfather clock still ticking, his log and journals ranged on the desk.

Even his slippers and smoking jacket set by the bed; crisp starched sheets tucked tight at the corners, the blankets arranged and neatly folded; Coffin's work.

The Bible rested in its usual place on the side table. The tasselled cord drawn between the pages revealed no clues – Isaiah 11:5–7, the passage he often recited at morning prayers, the one that bored us all – *the wolf also shall dwell with the lamb, the leopard shall lie down with the kid, the calf and the young lion and the fatling together; and a little child shall lead them. And the cow and the bear shall feed; their young ones shall lie down together; and the lion shall eat straw like the ox.*

Sir John lay back in his chair, plumply serene as if overtaken by an afternoon nap.

The surgeon held the captain's wrist. Cause of death, unfathomable, unknown, some time after midnight.

I think we gave up understanding before the ship's bell began its terrible lowing and the crew filed in and stood before the waxen mask. The fading blue eyes now closed. His sword and musket belted to his waist.

Tutt and Fitzjames prayed beside the bed where their captain now reclined, the fingers beginning to curl against the palm of his hands.

Pipes heralded Crozier into the darkened room, his mouth drawn in a snarl of disbelief – the irony, the ludicrous mischance of it all, that this should be his fate, in command at last.

The crew directed their gaze from the outstretched corpse to their new leader and back again.

I think we all wanted him to will the ship into a quiet oblivion, a slow settling into normality, soothed by chaste and noble lies, all well.

Crozier hovered uncertain, could offer no answer or words of consolation to the waiting expectant men.

Later I made my buffeting way on deck.

The sky was painted black, struck with silver papier-mâché stars, a Milky Way glitter of some Nativity play.

The sloping bluffs of King William Island were fake.

And the wind, whipping from the south, pumped by a theatrical storm machine, I refused to believe in.

Most nights in the library, I hear wild melodizing from the officers' mess. Lately they've been playing party games like children. They drink brandy, cheat at poker, dance breathless mincing quadrilles, quite out of step and all the while the young Coffin does violence to the Jewish harp.

Occasionally hearing their wild carousing, I've set down my book with a sigh, singed the candle between forefinger and thumb and followed the ropes up the companionway to investigate. When I open the door, I find the room deserted, not a sound.

Bedford Square. November 1851.

Six years have passed and another winter is upon us, sleet spilling from granite skies.

Captain Penny is back, Commander Philips, Captain Ross, Captain Austin, those brave souls sent by the Admiralty, the Americans, Captain de Haven and Dr Elisha Kent Kane all returned.

Penny and Philips call on me at once. Sophy ushers them upstairs where I wait in the Japan Room, my heart knocking against my chest, knowing that Beechey Island has been explored in full.

I allow Sophy to attend to the ceremony of pouring tea. I have not the strength. It is enough to control my agitated state, remain seated on the ottoman, dignified, poised. 'Thank you, my dear, that will be all,' I say in a firm voice, motioning my niece to the door.

With a moue of disappointment, she darts me a reproachful look, but as I have explained time and time again, I can't have her constant exclamations and interruptions, or worse still not understanding what is being said. I need to concentrate. I take a deep breath and focus on my guests.

Captain Penny and Commander Philips cut tall and imposing figures, their lean faces pitted by the sun. I have every faith in them.

These are the facts. Good gentlemen, set them down.

Penny and his crew scoured Beechey's windblown shores, discovered scraps of newspaper dated September 1844, a torn note with the words 'until called', ragged shreds of clothing, discarded mittens. In the shortening days of late summer they were prepared to admit defeat, when a search party let out a cry.

Scrambling over loose and rugged slopes, the men reached the crest of an isthmus where three graves lay side by side among a rubble of snow and slate. Facing Cape Riley, the wooden headboards were fashioned in the old Orthodox style. Their inscriptions bore the names of three young ratings from my husband's ships: John Torrington, stoker, aged twenty years, January 1, 1846; John Hartnell, able seaman, twenty-five years, January 4; and William Braine marine, thirty-two years, April 3.

Proof at last that for his first 1845 winter quarters,

my husband had sheltered in a small bay on the east side of Beechey Island.

Resting the cup in the palm of his rough raw-boned hand, Penny describes the place as breathing the quiet of an English country churchyard and even the desolation of the frozen zone had been carefully culled to mark the seamen's last home.

Close by, they came across the scattered remains of tenting sites, an armourer's forge, storehouses, a carpenter's workshop, and several shooting stations within a mile of the anchorage. Even a polar bear killed by one of the searchers revealed an earlier wound and the bullet retrieved from the beast's flesh clearly identified as having been fired from a rifle like those supplied to my husband.

Most strange among the relics, a high cairn of some seven hundred discarded tin cans, provisions, which on closer inspection, had been weighed with gravel, yet alas no document or record found.

'Since three of the crew, young, strong and able men, had expired within the first months of the voyage,' Penny declares, 'one may infer they were not enjoying the perfect health.'

Somehow I manage a polite nod.

He tells me the surgeon Dr Peter Sutherland believed important clues to their fate might be harboured within the tombs and proposed their exhumation.

'He called to have the graves opened,' he says, 'but as there seemed to be a feeling against this most important step, it was not reiterated.'

Commander Philips takes out a paper from his top pocket and spreads it out on the table before us.

'The surgeon's report, ma'am.'

Eagerly I scan the document written in neat copperplate.

Philips leans forward and begins to read out loud.

'The cause of Braine's death, which happened in April,' he says, 'might have been scurvy supervening upon some other disease. The first two deaths within four days of one another in January had probably been caused by accidents, such as frostbite or exposure to intense cold, or to diseases in the chest where there might have been some latent mischief before leaving England and which the intense winter conditions of November and December stimulated to a fatal termination.'

I fairly seethe with questions. 'Why weren't the bodies examined?' I ask. 'Surely they would have been in a high state of preservation in their frozen castings.'

I imagine the youths, lips drawn back from their teeth, oyster eyes of water ice, yet their features, the skin and hair and clothes as they had been six years ago on their last day of life.

Penny and the commander exchange glances.

'A hard season the crew had had of it,' Philips says. 'Exhuming the corpses of their fellow countrymen might have sparked a mutiny.' We sit in silence for a moment. The men head bowed as if in mournful prayer.

Had I been in their place, I would have given immediate orders to unearth the coffins with pickaxes and shovels, never mind the morbid sensibilities of the men. But I must accept the information these captains choose to pass my way. Already they've been debriefed by the Admiralty, their narrative pared and shaped into a sanitized account to be published tomorrow in the morning papers.

More tea, I say proffering the pot, but the good gentlemen desist. I decide to introduce another line of enquiry.

'How do you interpret the cairn of tin cans?'

'Perhaps,' Penny ventures, 'the preserved meats proved of an inferior quality.'

Food poisoning. My husband took such pride in Goldner's provisions. Top notch, he had said, one of the country's finest inventions. Had even recruited some French chef to prepare the meals for his officers. Forget the man's name, now.

'And why was no record deposited,' I ask, 'indicating the precise route the ships may have taken?'

At this, Penny lets out a long sigh. Philips folds away the surgeon's document.

'Evidence in the great pile of relics,' Penny begins, setting his cup on the lacquer tray, 'shows they might have left their winter encampment in a considerable hurry.'

Philips brings out another sheaf of paper.

'A list submitted to Admiralty House.'

He clears his throat:

Item one: an expensive pair of cashmere gloves, set beneath a stone to dry, belonging to Commander James Fitzjames.

Item two: four bearskins, each labelled for the Natural History Museum.

Item three: botanical specimens, bottles of sea grass, sassafras, shells apparently forgotten by the Observatory door.

Item four: reindeer and elk carcasses, no doubt intended to be winched aboard.

Item five: the smashed remains of barrels containing whale blubber, possibly lost against the ship's sides.

Item six – here Penny and his colleague look me straight in the eye.

Philips stoops and, searching in a pigskin holdall at his feet, lifts out a bundle of felt.

'Cutlery, my lady.'

I take the package from his outstretched hands, and carefully unwrap each one.

My husband's monogram engraved on tarnished handles, fish knives and spoons, the finds of Franklin's first encampment delivering the facts but not the history behind them. These objects will be sent to Greenwich and preserved beneath glass displays to perpetuate their eloquence and silence.

When the good gentlemen take their leave, I call Sophy, and as soon as all her eager questions have been answered we sift over every detail like prospectors sieving for gold: would Franklin have ventured into Regent's Inlet, explored the channel between North Somerset and Prince of Wales Island, probed to the southward of Banks Land or taken the ships between King William Land and the coast of Boothia? We conclude the latter the most likely.

And in the spring of 1846, conditions must have been favourable for the encampment was rapidly dismantled – quite a scramble, it seems: no officer would leave behind an expensive pair of cashmere gloves – or scientific collections, botanical specimens for the Royal Geographical Society in Kensington Gore. Not even time even to cache a cylinder, an Admiralty report, quite contrary to my husband's conscientious character.

Unless – Sophy and I return to the mysterious cairn and the cook my husband employed. What could this steward have been thinking of – seven hundred tins, enough to provision a second winter at least. Such a waste, we exclaim, didn't he know that the Royal Navy has survived on a scantier diet than that.

'His name is Canot,' Sophy says, fiercely buffing one of my husband's silver spoons with chamois leather dipped in polish. 'He replaced Richard Wall.'

Admiring her prodigious memory, I too recall a compact dapper man with an immaculately trimmed pencil moustache and dark inquisitive eyes, the quiet assurance fitting to someone of his profession. Although he seemed subdued, bemused even, following the purser about the ship's waist.

Clearly this Canot had never been to sea before. Yet surely my husband would have been against squandering the expedition's precious stores so early on in the mission. And as fresh game had been plentiful, evidenced by the shooting stations, the cook could have husbanded the supplies, Arctic fox or hare perhaps.

So Sophy and I fret and speculate until dawn.

Three men painstakingly buried, a cairn of cans laid waste – a portent, a narrative both told and withheld.

November 5th, 1852 marks the anniversary of our wedding day twenty-three years ago in that pretty Stanmore church.

I gaze at my reflection in the looking glass. The passing decades have not served me well. Fine vertical lines are beginning to appear around my mouth, the upper lip in particular, a look I have always found repellent among dowagers of a certain age. That is Jane, aged fifty-nine now. The mole on my chin admired in my youth as a beauty spot sprouts hairs, which most mornings have to be plucked. Soon my eyesight will fail and I'll no longer notice these whiskers and my appearance will frighten small children who will call me a witch. I am old and tired. I have problems with aching joints, my teeth, yet I am not too vain to arrange and rearrange my widow's veil so that it billows fetchingly about my face.

Still I am cheered by the moves from Admiralty House – a search expedition of three sailing ships and two steamers under the command of Sir Edward Belcher dispatched north of Barrow Strait with Wellington Channel the main objective. The officers splendid men, Kellett, McClintock, Pullen, Mecham, Nares.

And this afternoon, the American explorer, Dr Elisha Kane, will honour me with a visit.

He arrives very gaunt and grey, they say an Arctic night and an Arctic day can age a man more harshly than a year spent anywhere else in all the weary world.

Kane tells me that when my vessel the *Albert* and the *Advance* found themselves beset off Baffin Island, he could hear an organ grinding out 'The Garb of Old Gael', which in itself formed an entire orchestra. At first when he and his crew heard the tunes drifting across the ice, they believed they had entered some dreamlike state and the floes tinkled with the refrains of music-hall songs they remembered as boys. Kane set out with his sledge and dogs and to his astonishment came across the *Albert*, which he took to be a phantom ship, frost glistening like fish scales on the hulls. Bellot was the first officer to greet him. They embraced as long-lost friends.

Kane relates how he taught Bellot to stalk a seal in the Esquimaux manner, crawling on his belly and elbows, on another occasion he attempted to chase a bear around an inlet where Bellot and Captain Kennedy lay waiting with their muskets, only for the beast to gallop away across the distant hummocks.

He explains that Bellot had volunteered to lead four men in a hazardous trek along the frozen expanse of Wellington Channel, carrying dispatches for Belcher, whose ships lay embayed north of the straits.

The pack ice was melting rapidly and Bellot's party became trapped on a floe, which had splintered from the beach. Ever resourceful, they camped overnight. Early the next morning, Bellot proposed to reconnoitre the shrinking shorelines and stepped from the tent. 'As God protects us,' he assured his frightened men, 'not a hair of our heads will fall to the ground.'

I stifle a giggle at the quaint turn of phrase.

Kane pauses, studies me for a moment then resumes his narrative.

After five or six minutes had elapsed, no sign of the first officer, not a word, his companions rushed out after their leader. Scouring the floe, they espied Bellot's carved walnut walking stick drifting on the far side of a thirty-foot lead.

'They say he must have fallen through an opening fissure never to be seen again.'

Bellot dead. It can't be so.

In the silence that ensues, before I begin to feel the waves of desolation, which threaten to overpower me, I manage to confide in Kane that the brave and generous young man, whom I loved as a son, to whom I owe so much – died as he lived, a hero and a Christian.

Kane gives an understanding nod.

When Kane takes his leave, I express my eager anticipation of his forthcoming book, a work I assure him, which will be one of the most graphic, the most touching and the most eloquent histories of Arctic adventure.

Kane bows and promises a signed first edition. Somehow I am able to say and do all of this like an automaton, a wind-up doll, as if I need to hold on to these courtesies, for once the door closes behind him I will crumple and never find myself, never be Jane again.

It is as I had foretold – my tears turn to racking sobs, which I stifle with my fists, pressed hard against my face. I don't want Netty or Sophy to hear and run up the stairs, come to my aid and pretend all is fine, consoling me with the notion that Bellot will be writ large in the history books. He was a mere boy, a sweet, gentle boy, who needlessly died, slipped through an ice-crack with hardly a splash, a ripple before dark waters closed over. I imagine the bewildered terror in his eyes, the stick wrenched from an outstretched hand, the cap torn from his head, as he sinks beneath the deep sunless caverns, his short life unfurling like a pennant before him.

Adieu, my friend.

A draught of laudanum helps ease the pain but befuddles my thoughts. I dream I am young and beautiful again. Bellot and I are dancing the night away in that draughty Stromness hall, the indomitable Mrs Rae gazing on in the company of her son John. The rhythms of the waltz quicken and only he and I command the floor, and it seems we are flying, faster and faster to a resounding roar. Just as Bellot reaches towards me for a kiss, I age and shrivel, the smooth skin coarsens and withers and when I smile, he recoils from the blackened stumps in my mouth. 'Ah, Jane,' he whispers, 'what have you become.'

I wake to blood on the pillow and a strange taste coating my tongue. Rinsing with a pitcher of water, I reach for the spittoon – another tooth gone. Never mind – I'm becoming quite fond of Netty's quince jellies.

I summon Sophy to the Japan Room for the first time in a week since I received news of Bellot.

'A monument would be fitting tribute,' I begin, noticing that Sophy has suffered too in the wan face, the shadows at her temples.

'I will write to Sir Roderick Murchison to form a committee. And no expense shall be spared on the memorial.'

Sophy brightens.

Did I see Bellot as a hero – in truth I did not – the boy slipped, lost his footing, a grotesque accident but I shall make him one.

We discuss materials, I in favour of rose marble, Sophy granite. We will petition for a site at Westminster or Kensington Gore close to the Royal Geographical Society. An elegant plinth engraved with a frieze of the first officer leading his sledge party cracking the whip at a team of huskies.

I sleep well that night, no dreams – Bellot's sharp intake of breath, the black fissure widening.

The *Erebus*. 1848.

February – month of whiting and dabs

Today Crozier studies me intently as I set out his cut crystal glass, the decanters of whisky and brandy on the butler's tray.

'The Esquimaux have a good word for the darkest months,' he begins, '*perlerorneq* – it means to feel the weight of life, Canot.'

Outside the pack begins a throbbing howl, shuddering beneath the ship's hull. A violent gust of wind thrashes against the great stern window and the heavy chandeliers begin to sway as if we were pitched in a storm.

Crozier sighs. 'We don't have long to live,' he announces abruptly as if concluding some silent argument with himself. His eyes are feverish, blade-sharp.

Our commander frightens me when he talks like this.

Perlerorneq – they say that slumber first creeps up on you with a terrible foot-stumbling weariness, that you yearn to seek shelter in a soft cleft of snow, that all sensation, the fear, the cold disappears and you succumb to a deep dreamless sleep. Not a bad way to go, like drowning where your life flashes before you in a series of fractured upturned images as if viewed through a kaleidoscope.

Out of habit and because I don't want to brood on these thoughts, I start polishing the tarnished silverware in readiness for dinner that night.

'Stop fussing, man,' Crozier growls, 'and pour me a drink.'

We have lost the last vestige of our midday twilight and the days are alike except a vague glimmer on the sky that defines the hills to the south.

Serving grog on deck, a new coastline meets my eyes. The men marvel at a huge floe dislodged from our ship on the starboard side, leaving an exact impression, gangway stairs of ice-block masonry.

*

My cathedral is toppling, breaking up. My vaulting gargoyles, the arched roofs, crowned with ramparts, those hoary belfries fretted to mere cobwebs.

Down in the sick bay, Officer Tutt raves, senseless tirades, hour after hour.

His body reeks of urine, stale vomit, and something else, sour and metallic.

I set down a broth of beef extract and lift the spoon to Tutt's lips. He averts his face, mouth clamped like a child.

Goodsir hurries towards us.

'Hemiplegia, paralysis to one side,' he whispers. 'Says he has difficulty swallowing, complains of numbness. Sit by him a while, there's a good fellow.'

And he dashes off again.

I try to prop the officer against sweat-stained pillows. Even in my weakened state, he is light as a feather, feeble as a rag doll. You can count every rib on his chest and his hands and feet appear very large on such spidery emaciated limbs.

Even so, Tutt manages to turn his poor sunken head my way.

'That man,' he murmurs, 'is trying to poison me.'

'Come now, Mr Tutt,' I soothe, 'take a sip, just for me.'

But the officer lies inert and stares up at the bulwarks on the ceiling.

'Listen to me, Canot,' he says. 'I will not eat or drink anything the surgeon has prescribed.'

He glares at Goodsir's retreating form.

'He's devised some infernal machine – it emits a blue vapour contaminating us all.'

I remain silent. Stir the congealing soup.

'Say something, God damn you,' Tutt begins to retch, choking on bile. I hold a spittoon close to his chin and look away until he is done.

Sobbing, Tutt lifts one arm and follows the trajectory of some imaginary shape.

'Surely you can see it coiling around the atmosphere?'

'Calm yourself, sir.' I scan the room. Ranged in tight rows, sixteen men lost in the babbling delirium of their dreams.

'Don't be a fool, Canot, there it is plain.'

I don't have the patience for this. Am far from well myself. My gums bleed. My bones ache. The joints in my right hand swollen beyond recognition exactly where my school teacher caned me, that time he lost control.

'They plan to murder us.' Tutt clutches at my cloak.

I wonder if I should call Goodsir to my aid but he is gone. I should not be left alone like this.

With difficulty, Tutt raises himself from the mattress.

'Somewhere Goodsir has concealed his machine and is pumping Prussic acid into the sick bay. Can't you hear it hiss and squeal?'

I must remain rational, calm.

'Why only the other day, I overheard Crozier discuss mercy killings. The number of sick have to be reduced, his very words.'

I push back my chair and rise slowly to my feet.

'Goodnight, sir,' I say in a quiet tone. 'Time to take a nap.'

'We need you, Canot,' Tutt declares. 'You have to find where it is hidden and switch the damn thing off.'

Ignoring his invective, the obscenities hurled from his mouth, I hurry through the half-opened door.

I stand outside, trembling. I fear for the future. We are out of our right minds.

On deck a monotonous sound of nails hammered into wood. The ice is shifting, or the construction of Tutt's coffin perhaps.

Who knows?

Flares throw long shadows on the fractured angles of upturned hummocks, where the bear was discovered two days ago, wedged between two slabs of ice, his muzzle rubbed deep into the snow. Twice he had stopped to lie down during his death march – blood turning each spot into crimson-veined marble.

The creature will extend our rations – but frozen firm, the carcass has to be cut with a handsaw. I have hardly the strength and there are moments when I almost give up in despair.

All night, I sit by Tutt. Try to still those hands restlessly roaming, tweaking and pinching the sheets. At intervals, summoning all his strength, he points towards the ceiling, his eyes rolling back in his head. I hope the poisoned vapours have gone. There a smile flickers at those lips shrunk to a grimace.

Ah, he sighs. That's good, the cool rushing air, the beating of wings.

I count the seconds between each rasping intake of breath, the rattle deep in his throat. There is something obscene about this vigil. It is like watching Christ die on the cross. And it takes so long. Sometimes I drift away myself, wander the candlelit rooms of my childhood, or find myself with a lover, imagine pretty Jeanette at my side, then I wake and with a pang, remember. Kingdoms are clay – here is our space, rotting alive in the hull of this ship.

I glance at Tutt. He lies back, arms outstretched. Not a sound from that gaping mouth. With the utmost gentleness, I close his eyes.

The men stamp their feet. The crew struggle with picks and axes. In silence Tutt's body is lowered. Ship life resumes, hushed, conspiratorial, conducted in whispers.

Most days, ignoring the ache in my limbs, I stumble across the plains to inspect the fallen ramparts of my Rouen. From a new lagoon, I spot a whale blowing purple sprays into the night shine. Take a shot.

Strange despite the fissures and the gales, the men's sculptures remain, Queen Victoria as sharply defined as when she was first carved. Not even the sceptre has fallen. You can see every detail in the elephant she rides, the arched tusks, the ornate high-backed saddle engraved with pineapples and palms. Yet six feet away, behind the mermaids gracefully reclined, the life-sized chess pieces – menacing at times, the rooks and knights seem to move as I pick my way past – my beautiful cathedral reduced to mere rubble, the same blunt blocks which defeated poor Tutt.

I won't begin again. Could barely wield a shovel now. But I can still discern the eager prints of my toil trailing back and forth to the fire hole.

Seeing them I laugh, monstrous sound, hyena howls echoing in the silence. Even I have left a mark on this savage land – the scuffed boot soles of unaccommodated man.

Nearing the end as we are, I wonder what others will make of these memorials should a ship appear long after we have gone.

Bedford Square. January 12, 1854.

Almost nine years since my husband's expedition set out and I receive this – it cannot be so. Surely they would wait at least until Belcher's return?

I smooth the paper on the desk and read Sir James Graham's directions again – the names of the officers and the men of the *Erebus* and *Terror* will be removed from the books of the Admiralty on the 31st of March.

What can they be thinking of? This action is tantamount to announcing the legal death of my husband, an admission that the missing sailors had perished, precipitating an official proving of Franklin's will and the process of applying its provisions. I dread an appeal to the Chancery. Eleanor will be thrilled.

I must be strong and fight this to the last. I take up a pen and begin to write – *the decision is a presumption in the sight of God as it will be felt to be indecorous, not to say indecent in the eyes of men* – I pause and glance out of the window, dark sullen skies, grey sleet driving against the panes – *You must pardon me for speaking the truth, as I feel it.*

And the truth as I feel it, I want to say, is that I drove my husband into the Arctic. I am responsible for his fate. I, a mere wife, strode into Admiralty House and beguiled everyone from the clerks to the First and Second Secretaries with the persuasiveness of my tongue. And I confess, even I was surprised by the extent of my influence. Of course it helped that his colleagues were so reluctant to take command of the expedition they fairly rallied to Franklin's cause. Cheered him on with grand speeches and signed petitions.

I am aware from the moment we married that I changed the course of Franklin's life. Made him turn down Lord Glenelg's first offer of that pestilential post in Antigua, and the second, overseeing sheep stations in central New South Wales, Australia. Although the last appointment would have suited my husband well – like his Lincolnshire forebears he would have made an excellent farmer but I had other plans. Did not see Lady Franklin as a drover's wife.

So we accepted the Governorship of Van Diemen's Land – in hindsight the worst mistake on my part and for which I am paying now. The irony does not escape me that Montagu's successor, James Ebenezer Bicheno, who sailed into Hobart with Lord Stanley's papers of our dismissal in his hands, would have proved an ally and close friend. A placid, amiable man, a gourmand who enjoyed a glass of port, a cigar after his meals, Bicheno certainly had no intention of bothering himself beyond the call of duty by the noisome business of politics, unlike that viper Montagu. Bad timing all round. Put it this way, Bicheno came seven years too late to our doors.

Once installed in Bedford Square, I had a tarnished reputation to repair, a bloodied suit of armour to mend and polish.

I nagged and chivvied like a terrier at Franklin's heels. Think of it, I declared, the North-West Passage. And glancing up, he would give me an affectionate weary smile.

Poor Franklin, what have I done – how could I have sent such a man into the ice, old and defeated and so very fat around the belly?

Now the Admiralty has pronounced him dead, wiped his name from the active service records and promised in compensation a paltry widow's pension hoping I will accept the pittance and keep quiet.

Carefully I press the paper with a blotter – *I believe that my husband may yet be living,* I continue, *where your expeditions have never searched for him, in a quarter where my own little vessel, in the absence of any better means, would have endeavoured to look for him had you not denied me the means and facilities for doing so.*

The fire gutters in the grate. Outside the sleet thickens to snow, which never settles on the streets but turns to sludge the moment it falls.

You will not expect me, sir, I conclude, *to claim from the Admiralty the widow's pension, which you remind me is granted under certain regulations.*

Again I gaze out of the window – my little robin has not returned this year and the crumbs which I sprinkle on the sill are gobbled by starlings and pigeons. I am sick of shadows, and endlessly composing letters, the equivalent of a dozen novels at least.

As I lean forward to dip the quill in ink, I knock the candle from its holder and snatching it up, spill droplets of wax across my crêpe skirt. Furiously I scrub the stains with a handkerchief. I will never get the grease spots out – that's the trouble with black, it shows up every mark.

I return to my correspondence – reread the part alluding to the widow's pension and of course – why had I not seized on the thought before?

Pushing back my chair, I rise to my feet and hurry towards the inlaid walnut wardrobe, which had been mother's before she died.

I fling open the doors and such a sight meets my eyes. Bright colours, greens and pinks, my favourite combination, the evening dress I wore twenty-four years ago when presented to the King at the Brighton Pavilion ball and greatly admired by Mrs Fitzherbert – white lace over satin with a deep border of silver grapes and gold leaves, the emerald train trimmed in purple cord – gowns for every occasion, plain muslin at breakfast with a bonnet and shawl when promenading during the day; satin tea gowns, pale rose or daffodil-yellow, edged with tulle ribbon; an elaborate confection of floss silk and gauze, a diamond wreath and lappets to wear at supper, a headdress of ostrich plumes.

I unbutton my heavy widow's weeds, fumble with hooks and stays – the person who invented such things should have been called to account for wasting the time of women who have more urgent matters to attend to than getting in and out of their clothes. Franklin could shed his uniform in three minutes flat and have his nightshirt on and be in bed before I had even begun to struggle with the tight mother-of-pearl fastenings of my chemise.

Finally I stand in my undergarments, shivering slightly before the fire. I reach for an elegant number of lime-green damask with a broad pink band at the hem and around the sleeves. For hours I strut and preen, admire myself in the glass.

At sixty-three I have aged, I admit, the body sagged, the once graceful athletic limbs have long lost their strength, their muscle tone. Yet I have always prided myself in never having gained a pound of weight since I was a girl. Not that you would expect it in someone so harried and plagued as I. You should see Isabella, Parry's wife – the carthorse girth on her – the plump skin rolling in folds from her arms and neck. But I must not be unkind.

My fate has decreed that I suffer and slender I remain, my face more lined, leaner than I would have liked but one cannot ask for everything.

They declare Franklin dead. So I will display deep mourning no more, banished are the ebony taffeta and velvets, the veil stoically worn for almost a decade now. As I will explain to the press it would be acting a falsehood and gross hypocrisy on my part to wear black when I have not yet given up hope. I shall parade along the Strand in the brightest, gayest attire I can muster and expect the officers' wives to follow suit.

When she comes upstairs, Sophy is alarmed I can tell as I twirl in all my finery before her.

'Why, Aunt,' she exclaims, her hands flying in

dismay to her mouth. 'You look wonderful,' she says in a faltering voice.

Sometimes it does no harm to frighten Sophy a little. I motion her to the pianoforte. 'Play something, my dear,' I implore. 'While they declare Franklin dead, I intend to celebrate.'

Seated dutifully at the keys, Sophy begins the first refrains of a waltz. I return my gaze to the looking glass and inspect the greying hair.

'I need Netty's magic touch,' I say. 'I think russet will do – can you ask her to mix up a pomade?'

Sophy's shoulders tighten as she bends at her task, keen quickstepping notes that make me tap one foot in rhythm.

The following morning, Sophy sits beside me at the breakfast table and together we read the newspapers. On the front page of *The Times*, a sketch of Eleanor dressed in deep mourning, how predictable is that?

Now she has the audacity to suggest her stepmother has lost her wits when the only the other day a crowd applauded me as I walked across Bedford Square.

How I tremble for her mind, she writes, *Lady Franklin is fast losing public sympathy by her strange conduct.*

Adding – *I think she could be influenced for good again, were Sophy not with her.*

My niece and I exchange glances.

But she keeps Sophy up to her determination instead of encouraging softer feelings.

As to Franklin's will, the darling daughter opines – *If my dear father could have been advised on the subject, he would have said, 'Follow the Government on this.' I am quite convinced, and we intend to act as we think he would have wished.*

'You gave Uncle everything,' Sophy declares rising to her feet. 'But for your generosity, your own fortune, or rather the remnant of it, would not now be passing to the Gells.'

I do love my clever niece, who mostly manages to say the right thing to please. And she too is endeavouring to show support. The bright citrus gown she wears could be quite fetching in a more flattering light.

Part Two

From the mutilated state of many of the corpses and the contents of the kettles, it is evident that our wretched countrymen had been driven to the last resource – cannibalism – as a means of prolonging existence.

John Rae, *The Times*, October 23, 1854

Bedford Square. 1854.

Autumn and the streets are sleek and slippery with leaves raked from the sycamores by heavy rains. It is not safe to walk out today.

Besides, I need to husband all my strength. So I sit in the Japan Room, regal, poised and wait. For a decade now I have been waiting.

Soon John Rae will be here and graciously I must greet him and listen to the man's vile calumny, which threatens to destroy Franklin's reputation.

Will he look at me when he describes the cook's knife, the discarded pots and kettles, relates the swaggering narratives of Esquimaux savages?

I have yet to see the new relics, the broken watches, telescopes and compasses, frayed remnants of gold braid. These articles have been packed and dispatched to Greenwich where I will have to view them through a glass cabinet unable to touch Franklin's order of the

KCH inscribed on a round silver plate, the star and badge of the Royal Guelphic Order dated 1835 and bearing the motto – Nec aspera terrent – which makes me weep and smile in turns – *Difficulties do not terrify*.

Indeed.

Ah, there's a ring at the door, this Hudson Bay Company voyager has arrived, the man on whom I had pinned all my hopes and written asking whether the mouth of the Great Fish River should be examined. Footsteps up the stairs. Sophy's voice along the corridor and my niece hovers ever hopeful beside the tall rangy figure of Dr John Rae.

'Thank you, Sophy, that will be all,' I say.

He still sports a full Arctic beard like a trophy, a matted brown mane which hangs down to his lean belly. From beneath tangled brows, his eyes gleam ice blue just like his mother's.

I motion him to a chair. After all, I have read and reread his front-page report in *The Times*. What more can be said, the profanity is out.

Rae bows and scratches the tips of my fingers with his prickly moustache. Had he spoken to me plain, confided his findings before seeking an appointment with the Admiralty, I might have forgiven him. Pity, for I had once admired this polar professional. Had even enjoyed a glass of cherry brandy with his mother.

Instead he allowed this ghoulish second-hand information to be published for all to read.

Rae, the dutiful explorer, takes a seat, bending and arranging his long angular limbs like a camel lowering itself onto desert sands. He casts me a glance both curious and triumphant as if he were a schoolboy expecting a prize. Not from me, he won't. And I will object if he receives the ten thousand pound Admiralty reward for conclusive information upon Franklin's fate. Do everything within my power to obstruct him in this desire.

Dr Rae seems uncertain how to begin. He twists and turns in his chair, clears his throat several times. *My dear Lady Franklin*, is a start.

There is Esquimaux blood in these Raes. I can testify to that for he claims he *conversed* with the savages, his very words, *conducted interviews* as he presided like a magistrate in his tent, gleaning facts from eyewitness accounts.

It was spring 1850, the natives say, when they saw a party of white men, *kabloonans*, alive, some forty of them, dragging a boat from the north of King William Land, indicating by sign language that their ship had been crushed by the ice. They were travelling southward to find deer to shoot, and later the same year thirty corpses were discovered near the estuary of the

Great Fish River sprawled in tents or on the ground, others seeking shelter in the overturned boat.

Rae talks about these Esquimaux with reverential pride as if these people mattered, as if he cared and believed in them. To secure information, he had offered substantial rewards – bribes, liquor no doubt – so they could blabber to their heart's delight.

There was no mention of an elderly man among them and had Franklin survived the wreck of his vessel, he would not have ventured for the River, knowing from his own experience what little chance the Barren Lands afforded of survival. Of that I am assured.

My husband is dead. Cannot be alive. I have known it since Rae's return.

Yet still I harbour hope there may still be survivors and records recovered in time.

Speech over, Rae leans back with a sigh.

'Did you see the corpses for yourself?' I ask, surprised at my composure. 'And the kettles of human flesh?' I force myself to add.

Rae shakes his shaggy leonine head.

'Have you anything to support your evidence other than the word of natives? How can you rely on mere hearsay?'

Oh, he fairly winces at that.

'My dear lady,' he tries to object.

Still I continue.

'Your relics might have convinced you my husband is dead, and a number of his crew have perished, but I will never accept the outrageous calumny that comes with them. Besides you have not recovered anything that could not have been stolen by thieving tribes.'

On and on I persist. Until, finally, Rae rises to his feet and begins to pace the room.

'I insist,' he declares, 'that I know the truth when I hear it.'

'Why did you not check the evidence yourself?' I am in my stride and in some way I pity him for he is lamentably easy to checkmate.

Rae's strong broad shoulders seem to sag.

'Examining the corpses and relics would have meant staying in the region for another winter.'

His voice is high-pitched, querulous, the colour rising in his throat. Just like poor Franklin baited and tormented in the whispering corridors of Government House.

'I felt it was more important to bring the news home.'

'And collect the Admiralty reward,' I offer in an even, neutral tone, a manner which always without fail exasperated Montagu.

'Lady Franklin,' he replies, 'I did not write my report

for a newspaper but as private correspondence to the Admiralty.'

Now it is my turn to rise to my feet.

'Sir,' I say, 'it would have been better not to have committed such libel to paper at all.'

Ah, Jane, this persona I have created, feeble and frail in body yet brave and strong of mind.

'Dr John Rae,' I declare. 'Are you prepared to publicly retract your vile infamy before this matter is further sensationalized by the press?'

At a loss, Rae glances my way, clearly baffled.

'Consider this,' I explain, 'if the choice lay between believing an Esquimaux or the moral fortitude of British explorers, which would the public choose? Think on it.'

'I am prepared, madam,' he concedes at last, 'to lead an expedition to search for further evidence in any vessel Lady Franklin might have at her disposal.'

Why, the cheek of it!

'And what makes you believe I would enlist you as commander of such a venture?'

Rae gives a curt nod and takes his leave. Marching out of the door, he almost knocks Sophy off her feet as she crouches at the keyhole.

'Well?' she demands, after curtseying to Rae's retreating form.

'For the sake of my husband and his men, I intend to ruin him, of course.'

Later I will shed tears. Grief is what England wants and I must deliver a flood. Nine years of false hope and Franklin is dead. I know it.

I will not lament the past. Look into the future instead. At least Rae has proved without doubt that my husband carried out his instructions. I shall petition an expedition to be dispatched at once. If I can't save Franklin, I will champion him as a hero for the sacrifice not to have been in vain. He would be sixty-eight years old by now. God rest his soul.

The *Erebus*. 1848.

March – month of pemmican and hard tack

Thirty-eight sick and dying men slumped below.

Carried on a stretcher, Fitzjames orders cannon to be fired for the advancing ships. He passes me the glass.

'The masts, yards, gaffs, everything but the bowsprits can be made out quite distinctly,' he declares.

Fitzjames orders an expedition to make contact with the man in the black cloak seen motionless on the north-western floes.

'Look, he waves,' he shouts.

I examine the snow plains, virgin, without one single speck.

Venturing again into the storerooms, those chilled cavernous vaults filled with echoes, I decide to reserve the last of the pemmican – two barrels – and the fresh bear steaks for Crozier, which I will sauté in a smear of lard for I've made it my mission that Crozier will be kept level-headed and alive.

Although our leader barely notices the fare I place before him, gobbles it down in a couple of mouthfuls like a dog.

I creep past the bread bins, Coffin's lair. I can smell his nest from here. Lifting the taper, I espy him curled on worn sacking, surrounded by the gnawed white bones of his ossuary. Hunger and cold show their worst effects in the pallor of his aged emaciated skin. I pause and listen to the sharp rise and fall of his breath. He sleeps, thank God.

I wish I could lead him from this place across this blue glazed porcelain ice to the kitchen of my childhood – prepare him a soft-boiled egg, buttered toast cut into soldiers placed on a tray on his lap. I would love to watch the boy dip warm bread into the golden dripping yolk, embers spitting from the grate as my nurse bustled about and drew the brocaded curtains tight against the gathering night. Coffin deserves more than this.

I find myself increasingly attentive to Crozier's comforts and desires – with a tenderness which surprises me at times, ensuring as best I can in this dripping den that all is satisfactory, ship-shape for our commander, who pores over the charts and anaesthetizes his despair with each decanter I unstopper.

April he tells me is the most propitious month to abandon the vessels.

'The weeks of late spring,' he explains, stabbing the mouth of the Great Fish River with the point of a sharpened quill. 'When the ice is still firm underfoot and before the warmer weather of midsummer breaks the floes creating soft slush and dangerous open lanes.'

When he talks like this, I continue to chivvy and fuss, plumping the cushions, mopping the floors like an old sea captain's wife.

'A desperate gamble, Canot, I know.

'Yet I have every confidence,' he continues, 'that we will walk to freedom in the end.'

This morning, accepting the invitation to share an aperitif of cognac, doing our best to ignore the carousing from Fitzjames and the officers in the mess, Crozier lifts his great mane of a head from his paperwork, gazes my way and sighs.

'Have you noticed, Canot,' he whispers, 'that some of the men harbour dangerous looks. This hunger for fresh meat disturbs their brains and I cannot but fear that they are contemplating crime.'

In the deep shadows of the room and the uneasy flickering of the spent candlelight, we seem diminished. Two wizened men staring at each other, almost invisible in the darkness.

The past is of no use to us now. Nor the future – the march to Fish River.

No one at home would believe how exhausting it is to trek without baggage even the short stretch to the sculpture meadows, over terrain that slips from your feet, surmounting obstacles created by the gales and snow, the excessive cold, one part of your body in a sweat, the other blinded by a fog which hinders the route you are following for you cannot have the compass constantly in your hand. I have every faith in Crozier, indeed I believe I love the man – but this expedition to the River is nothing but madness and will be the undoing of us all.

Bedford Square. December 1854.

Poor Rae. I warned him. Told him to retract. Any fool could tell how the public would react. I flick through the morning newspapers. Articles, pamphlets and letters to the press expressing a shocked refusal to believe Rae's monstrous implications, the gross moral collapse of the flower of the British navy.

All savages are liars, claims a *Times* editorial.

I should be content with that – yet I have other supporters rallying to the cause. Again I inspect the card propped against the teapot, reread the immaculate copperplate hand, *Lady Franklin I shall come to you at once*. Signed *Charles Dickens*.

I am flattered. Already Sophy has ordered his latest novel, *Hard Times*.

In preparation of his visit, I have Netty sorting through my gowns. For on the subject of my wardrobe, I confess I remain unresolved.

My husband is dead. I know that now. To return to widow's weeds would be perceived as an affirmation of Rae's account; yet to continue with my gay pinks and greens might strike the wrong note with a nation intent on mourning. How can the simplest task of getting dressed prove so difficult? Sophy suggests I opt for a neutral dove-grey. With a gauze veil, perhaps. I dare not even think of Eleanor stuck for months in black.

She too has written hoping that now faced with evidence her dear Papa has expired, the family could come together in peace and love and *Jane would finally forgive us as we heartily forgive you.*

Immediately I replied, *I care but little for the money now that it is no longer wanted for my dearest husband's life, and should have valued it chiefly for your sakes, if you would have trusted me.*

So far I have not received a word but have other matters to attend – namely this afternoon's appointment with the greatest writer in England. I want Dr John Rae repudiated and only Mr Dickens can accomplish that task.

A diminutive, tousle-haired, irritable man, Dickens restlessly drums his fingers on the armrest of the divan as I elaborate over Rae's report, studying me all the while with animated jet-black eyes, which so I am told exert such a devastating influence on the fairer sex. Yet fail to hold me spellbound for I dislike the sensation of being watched, being a keen observer myself.

The intensity of his gaze is unsettling and I wonder if he has me pinned in his mind for a cameo appearance, a caricature, Mrs Sparsit perhaps. Despite his irascibility, the persistent scowl, Dickens is a desperately busy man – not one to waste his time – and I must beguile and charm, make him feel the appointment is worthwhile.

First I cast Rae outside the gallant band of gentlemen naval officers. Present him instead as something of an opportunist, a rough diamond by way of contrast to the noble conduct of my husband, Sir John Franklin, the youthful courage of his officers, De Voeux, Fitzjames and Gore, and Bellot, my brave lost surrogate son.

I must intrigue and arouse his disgust in Rae's false allegations – lingering on the sharpened cook's knife, the kettle pots, the discarded gristle of human flesh.

'Why, the very notion is unthinkable,' Dickens declares. 'Pray continue, Lady Franklin.'

I suggest that indeed my husband's men might well have been murdered by the Esquimaux themselves for it is impossible to estimate the character of any race of savages—

I glance up. Perhaps I have gone too far, my language too strong.

But Dickens leans forward, entranced.

'Quite so,' he says. 'We believe every savage to be in his heart covetous, treacherous and cruel.'

By *we*, he means England, and our young Queen.

Inwardly I rejoice, for once again I have won another victory for my husband and his men.

When he takes his leave, Dickens kisses my hand, assuring me that now he was rather strong on voyages and cannibalism, he might consider an interesting little paper for the next issue of his magazine, *Household Words*.

'I can see no reason to believe,' he murmurs, 'that our wretched countrymen had been driven to the last resource.'

From the beginning poor Rae never stood a chance.

Not one but a mighty two-part series published in *Household Words*, holding the nation in thrall. An article of faith liberally spiced with blood-curdling stories for the entertainment of his readers, a sell-out performance vindicated by the great clamour of people queuing in Wellington Street north of the Strand for the Christmas instalment.

Never underestimate a true wordsmith, I tell Sophy, reading the article out loud.

We submit that the memory of the lost Arctic voyagers is placed, by reason and experience, high above the taint of this so-easily allowed connection; and that the noble conduct and example of such men, and of their own great leader himself, under similar endurances, belies it, and outweighs by the weight of the whole universe the chatter of a gross handful of uncivilised people, with a domesticity of blood and blubber.

'Domesticity of blood and blubber, such rhetoric is enough to make one swoon,' Sophy says.

I look at her. At forty-two, Charles Dickens would have made quite a match for they say his wife is fat and rather red in the face.

Adjusting my pince-nez, I read on.

– *Even the sight of cooked and dissevered human bodies among this or that tattooed tribe is not proof. Such appropriate offerings to their barbarous, wide-mouthed, goggle-eyed gods, savages have been often seen and known to make.*

'Bravo,' Sophy exclaims. 'I shall buy all Mr Dickens' novels.'

Later that night, how my spirits wane at the shortened days, the sun's swift four o'clock descent – I sit at my desk by the fire and begin to compile if I say so myself a clever missive to Admiralty House.

Though it is my humble hope and prayer that the Government of my country will themselves complete the work they have begun –

I gaze out of the window unsure of how to continue, when a stray phrase floats across my mind – *though I have the body of a woman, I have the heart and stomach of a man*. Well put, the Tilbury speech, Elizabeth I.

A flash of steady blue eyes, braided gold threading russet hair, flawless alabaster skin, a slender monarch determined to rouse the iron will within her.

And so, sharpening my pen, I transcribe the centuries:

And not leave it to a weak and helpless woman to attempt the doing that imperfectly, which they themselves can do so easily and well.

Yet if need be, such is my painful resolve, God helping me.

The *Erebus*. 1848.

March 20th – the vernal equinox

Nine officers. Fifteen crew. All dead. Our commander wanders the deck like a sick bear groaning.

No timber for the coffins.

This morning I hear a white whale singing, unfathomable note, one long under-ocean whistle followed by deep yodelling melodies of a Tyrolean kind.

Bivouacked in the library, I try and concentrate on *Gulliver's Travels*.

Why is that every book I choose taunts me with a beach, castaways washed on tropical shores, revived by a fierce noon sun, their ragged clothes dried in no time.

When I turn the page, the wick gutters in its tallow stub and seems to expire with the slightest movement.

Once again smothered in pitch-blackness, something creeps over my foot. I give out a feeble kick.

I reach for the candle in my pocket, smooth and tapered as a magician's wand. I am tempted. For an eternity I wrestle with myself, enclose the tinderbox in the palm of my hand. Ah for sharp scent of sulphur and the brief illumination of our world again.

A minute at the most, sixty dazzling seconds are all I ask.

The moment the thought enters my mind I am tempted to laugh.

Burn the books. Don't be daft.

Seventeen thousand volumes glazed with ice.

Set my galley stove ablaze.

Where to start?

The Pickwick Papers, tattered editions of *Punch*, which no one bothers to read any more? Those periodicals piled high in the cobwebbed corners of water closets, daily shredded from their spines. Perhaps one arresting paragraph perused; even speculations about our own fates considered before the final scrunch and wipe, flushed into a network of sewers tunnelled beneath the Thames.

Burn Punch.

Harlequin clown.

Burn Judy, his wife.

Let them burn.

At first a green flicker shoots upwards before bursting into flames. I smile when I see the lovely colour spreading so fast. Milton, Shakespeare, Dante. I rake the shelves – Donne, Marvell, Chaucer's pilgrims, the Wife of Bath in all her gap-toothed crimson glory, roaring behind tapestried curtains, Bunyan's itinerants showering cinders against the ceiling, the calfskin and vellum bindings unfurling.

A yellow-red conflagration fills the room like the burnished interior of a stone cathedral when all the candelabras at vespers are lit. The flames crackle and flare so fierce that I have to turn away lest my clothes are scorched. Yet the fire breathes life into my tired flesh, the chilled aching bones. Poor monster brought naked and panting forth with bellows and steam.

I sit alone in the darkness. Tears course my cheeks. I wipe them with the back of my sleeve. I must not give way, surrender to the shadow plays of my mind.

Burn the books. You must be mad, Canot.

You could be court-martialled for less than this.

The library. Sacred vault of contemplation and learning, ancestral song lines of thanes, hymns, odes and ballads the touchstone, the very ballast to civilization, ramparts of words raised against Esquimaux savages. This narrow cell is all we have, spider threads to the known world.

Bedford Square. 1856.

May, and the hyacinths are out in Netty's pretty terra-cotta pots, which she arranged on the sill insisting that – have patience, my lady – they would bring good cheer. And she was right. Just the sight of those tightly bunched pink and purple whorls gives me hope for another expedition, for the future. Their fragrance drifting through the half-opened window reminds me of my youth, when I was a girl, staying with some cousin in Hertfordshire and I wandered the woods behind the house, my arms full, gathering great wet bunches of bluebells and hyacinths, inhaling a sweet sap scent which made me feel alive.

Belcher has returned with nothing to report except the abandonment of all five of his ships. How can he show his face in public? Yet he struts like a lord to his club in Pall Mall.

Then there is a Captain McClure of the *Investigator*

who insists he has discovered a navigable North-West strait after sledging across frozen seas to seek sanctuary in the *Resolute*, one of Belcher's stricken vessels.

Why these explorers sail into port panting after prizes and money with the original quest to save my husband forgotten. Tirelessly I send missives rejecting McClure's 'walk a Passage' claim but find myself opposed on every front. Instead the committee declares beyond doubt this brave captain deserves the distinguished honour of being the first to perform the actual passage between the great oceans that encircle our globe – and other such nonsense. Ten thousand pounds squandered on the man.

All of which require further counter arguments, which keep Sophy and me up at night, shivering in our shawls as the embers glow grey in the grate. Surely, I write, it is Sir John Franklin, and not this McClure, who deserves the laurels for forging the passage's last link.

I will not desist – nor retire to the comfort of my bed until I have dictated: *What secrets may be hidden within those wrecked or stranded ships we know not – what may be buried in the graves of our unhappy countrymen or in caches not yet discovered we have yet to learn.*

Sophy and I have been going over the paperwork. If I sold out all our capital, including property in Van Diemen's Land, I could spare ten thousand pounds for the loan of a ship with stores and permission for one of the naval volunteers to command it.

And I have my eye on such a vessel. I have asked Mr Coppin to inspect a schooner-rigged steam yacht, the *Fox*, the property of Sir Richard Sutton, who has recently died, strip her fancy furnishings and equip her for Arctic service.

I confided in Coppin my preference for a British commander – for his sake, not my own.

Coppin has recommended Francis Leopold McClintock.

Expert sledger, he said, known for a persevering nature.

I like and know this capable and experienced officer. He sailed with Captain Ross, Captain Austin and lately most unfortunately with the scoundrel Belcher. If he survived that coward's command, anything can be achieved.

And McClintock has proved admirable indeed, such gallantry and enthusiasm. Accepting the position, he wrote expressing his concern that Lady Franklin must not be encouraged to sacrifice her fortune, for in his view I have always done too much. Willingly he presented himself as my obedient servant submitting to my every instruction and so on.

I wired in reply – your leave is granted; the *Fox* is mine, the refit will commence immediately.

Outlining three objectives, the rescue of possible survivors, the recovery of records and the confirmation of Franklin's claim to the discovery of the North-West Passage.

I also told him that a portion of my legacy remained intact, for three thousand pounds had been raised by subscriptions from sympathizers.

Fondly, I reread the list of names, thirteen Arctic officers, W. M. Thackeray, and Dr P. M. Roget, who at seventy-eight must surely care for his Jane from time to time.

Wearily Sophy and I set the table in order, Sophy helping me seal and fold each letter for Netty to take to Admiralty House.

Dear sweet Sophy. I reach for her hand. Who would have thought all those years back in Van Diemen's Land we should grow old and fretful together like husband and wife?

The fire has gone out. A soft pink light dapples mackerel skies. Arms entwined, we shuffle across the room, closing the door gently behind us, before the quick familiar kiss on the cheek and our separate ways to bed. As I recline beneath starched ironed sheets, turning my aching head this way and that, seeking respite among satin bolsters and pillows, I wonder how an entire decade can have passed, the two of us living this strangely cocooned spinster's life.

I must not shed tears when the *Fox* sails into the Pentland Firth. The cause at last is as secure as human means can make it.

Yet the prospect of the long wait, idling the empty hours, another harsh winter, the predictable social rounds, Bath, Ascot, Brighton, Leamington Spa fills me with despond.

Sophy and I must restore our spirits, perhaps a journey to Constantinople or the Holy Land with the view of fortifying ourselves for Captain McClintock's return.

We must prepare at once and Netty shall accompany us.

I am down to my last opium phial, which will tide me through the hour, when I wake with a sense of dread, of not having perhaps behaved to others – dear John, Sophy – as well as I should.

The *Erebus*. 1848.

Holy Saturday – April 22

I open the last keg of brandy, which ceremoniously I decant.

Crozier sits at his desk with the exhausted resignation of a condemned man.

Again he riffles through Back's account of the Great Fish River, which by his estimate lies some two hundred and fifty miles from our anchorage.

'Once we reach the mouth of the estuary,' our commander explains, 'we can hope to trek some seven hundred miles towards sanctuary at Fort Resolution on Slave Lake.'

Crozier smoothes a dog-eared page and begins to read out loud – *the river punctuated with a succession of dangerous rapids and waterfalls traces a violent and tortuous course running through a desolate stretch of country, the Barren Lands.*

Gratefully he seizes the glass I set by his side.

'However,' he declares, 'Back does state that the territory around the estuary will provide a source of game teeming with caribou, gulls and salmon.'

At the prospect, Crozier licks his lips.

'A gamble, Canot,' he murmurs. 'Another option is to head north to Fury Beach on Prince Regent's Inlet where twenty years ago Parry and I stockpiled tons of provisions from our wrecked vessel, the *Fury*. This cache would sustain us for several months and once revived I could follow the example of John Ross' – here Crozier smiles – 'who camped there in 1833 before leading his men towards Lancaster Sound, where they were rescued by a passing ship.'

We ignore the enraged shouts from the officers' mess, the shrieks of the Jewish harp.

'Yet – ' Crozier continues, 'shortly before leaving Deptford, rumours were circulating among the Admiralty that rogue whalers planned to salvage the *Fury*'s stores and sell them for quick profit.'

He closes the book and drums his fingers on the gilt leather spine staring ahead as if awaiting an answer.

Perhaps for the last time, I rearrange the chinaware, polish the engraved cutlery and refill the commander's glass.

For several days now the ice has been conspiratorially quiet, a mocking silence, defying us to venture outside.

'Which is it to be, Canot,' Crozier says taking a sovereign from his pocket and placing it on the table before him, 'north or south?'

With impatience he beckons me to his side. 'For God's sake stop fussing, man.'

Dutifully I fold a serviette through its silver ring, place it on the dresser and walk towards the desk.

Crozier spins the coin, catches it and flips it over on his wrist.

'Well,' he enquires, looking at me intently, 'heads or tails?'

From somewhere I hear the sound of drums and flutes, as if a pageant or a theatrical were about to begin. I remember the tambourine-playing gypsies of my youth and those wild high-stepping Breton girls, dressed in all their embroidered finery, bells tinkling from scarlet ribbons plaited in their braids as they skipped round and around a May pole at our village fair. Watching from behind my nurse's skirts, how I longed for the urgency of their kisses against my brow.

'Well, answer me,' Crozier calls, his voice distant rousing me from a dream, which I need to prolong for it to become real.

'Heads or tails, north or south?'

I imagine Coffin faltering behind a ragged line of men desperately dragging the unwieldy load, the long boats piled high with all the paraphernalia of *home*, changes of woollen uniforms and navy boots, the steel runners of the sledges buckling against rippled drifts of frozen snow.

'You are keeping me waiting, Canot.'

I, a mere cook, should not be drawn in and interrogated like this.

'Tails,' I say.

Crozier lifts his hand, studies the coin and lets out a sigh.

'Back's Great Fish River it is.'

'Best of three, sir,' I suggest.

Crozier regards me with contempt.

'I fail to see the point,' he murmurs, slipping the sovereign into his pocket.

Prepare to evacuate the vessels. What to take? What to leave behind?

In the library I run my hand along the shelves – *The Vicar of Wakefield*, perhaps.

The crew ready the whale boats with all their remaining strength; heaving the four cutters onto sleds fashioned in heavy elm and oak plundered from the ship's planks. I can hear their cries shrilling across the ice, Crozier marching back and forth screaming instructions.

I must inventory the provisions. Crozier's orders – calculate the last of the flour to be baked into hard biscuit, beef and herring to be scooped from their weighty casks, covered with salt and packed into lighter sacks, rum decanted into smaller kegs, rolled oats, dried peas, lentils, salt and sugar to be carefully wrapped in canvas, the remnants of Goldner's detestable preserved meats to be stewed in the steep pot. And so on.

Someone should inform him we are not up to the task.

I find myself leaning vertiginous against one of the cod barrels, phlegm curdling my lungs, bile rising in my throat.

I cast my eye over the stores, what to take, what to leave behind.

Chocolate of the dark rich bitter cooking kind in one-ounce lead-foil squares; caddies of fragrant loose tea, the finest from Darjeeling; cases of Havana cigars; soaps perfumed with attar of roses; porcelain dinner plates; candlesticks, mother-of-pearl medicine chests, monogrammed hair brushes, pens, sealing wax, toothpaste, jars of pomade.

And books of course, journals, all those tender letters written home. How can one let them fall into the hands of Esquimaux tribes?

From somewhere, a low whistle, Coffin slinking among the shadows.

Where are you? I shout, angry with him now.

I follow a sound of whispering rising from one recessed corner.

Coffin, I plead.

When I roll a barrel, a stream of vermin pours forth across the floor as if a patchwork fur cloak had been suddenly flung down.

Enter Carabosse followed by her retinue of rats.

The boy's laugher rattles the darkness, mocking and profane.

You shall prick your finger on a spinning wheel and die, die, die.

I back away from the shelves and tiptoe out of the storerooms without a glance, a single word.

On my way to the galley, I pause outside the purser's quarters.

Osmer, I call.

Silence.

I press my head against the cold clammy timber.

Osmer?

And there it is, the whirl and click of a deck spliced in his expert hand.

Gently I push open the door and survey his cabin in the brief flare of my taper.

Strewn on the desk, a pack of cards riffled and lifted by the wind. As I approach, a nine of spades and the Queen of Hearts skim at my feet, blown by a draught rushing beneath the threshold. I study the empty bottle of whisky, a dusty tumbler, the slight dent in rumpled blankets where Osmer had last slept. Sweet dreams.

In the galley, I think I hear rain, a great hammering overhead. The thaw has arrived and sends me tearful, stumbling on deck.

A steady unwavering line of snow geese flying north, purposeful, intent, the steady creak of their wings like the flap of linen on a windblown clothes line. I watch them soar in their thousands, spreading against the fractured sunlight, a brilliant, impeccable whiteness, opaque and without shadow.

Fitzjames comes running through the waist firing endless rounds of shot into the slate-blue air. Strangely, not one bird drops to the ground. It is as if each flock were part of something larger than itself, filling the skies in seamless currents, as far as the eye can reach, one fluid movement, invisible yet everywhere.

For two days and nights, the birds fly past, a constant ticking stream, we can hear their cries, a rising cheer from a far-off crowd.

Such a ball as you have never seen. Fitzjames drunk on champagne, Fairholme teeters, trips on the damask hem of his gown. Reluctant butler, I serve champagne, first to the ladies, then to the gents. Coffin winds the hand organ. Officers and gentlemen lining for the waltz. Toasts to Britannia. Votes for the ice queen. Nominations for the Emperor and Empress of the Straits.

The Admiralty would be proud at such a spectacle.

Four cannon shots. One by one, the men strain at the ropes, each in harness like a pack of dogs. Crozier at the lead, his head bent against the wind, cracking his whip, urging his crew on.

I stand alone in the great stern cabin.

One hundred souls haul the ship's boats crammed fit to bursting across the skating ground.

I scan the rink for Coffin, could that be him, the slender figure, flailing behind, cloaked in fox fur, dancing to some half-remembered jig, the refrains of a fiddle played in his mind.

Out of habit, I fold the napkins. Set the table as if I were serving our commander. Fill Crozier's tumbler – cheap brandy from Goodsir the surgeon's medicinal stocks. I survey the room, the furniture gleams, the chinaware ranged on the dresser, all in order. I stack the papers on Crozier's desk. I must stow these documents in the bolted recesses of his safe.

Should anyone—

Crozier guides his straggling crew through the sculpture grounds. I almost wave, watching them go.

Bagnères Bigorre. September 1859.

Netty endured, God bless her soul. At my insistence, she scrubbed and laundered our muddied clothes each evening, supervised without complaint the cooking arrangements of the next encampment, assembled the brass headstand of my travelling bed, and learned to tweak the mosquito nets just so to my satisfaction.

She even resigned herself to riding out astride most mornings.

'It really is the safest way,' I would assure her as she placed one hesitant foot on the clasped hands of our guide and heaved herself onto her obstinate mule.

Besides, I was tempted to add, the spectacle of three English women perched side-saddle on a pack of donkeys would simply be absurd. Not to mention perilous in high mountainous regions.

Always I led the way, keeping pace with our guide while Sophy and Netty trotted behind, exchanging the latest in calloused heels and blisters, the efficacies of ointments and plasters.

How could they grumble when they are both younger than me?

So now by way of a truce we find ourselves in this dull yet pleasant spa, Bagnères Bigorre, western France, the snow-capped Pyrenees laid out all before us. I have my eye on the Pic du Midi, which at ten thousand feet unveils one of the most celebrated vistas in Europe.

Over breakfast I confide my plan to Sophy. 'We can easily achieve the summit with a chaise à porteurs,' I say, 'then make the descent by foot. We will have to hurry though not to be overtaken by evening mists rolling through the valley.'

At the next table, two French ladies glance our way. I hope they haven't recognized who I am, expect me to answer awkward questions about my husband's fate, which is why I prefer to travel remoter lands incognito.

There's a commotion in the vestibule, a flurry of liveried uniforms hurrying to the door and a courier brandishing a paper, his boots and coat splashed with mud.

I rise to the cry *Dépêche Télégraphique* and the hotel proprietor striding across the breakfast room towards us. The ladies beside us gasp.

I can barely tear open the dispatch.

Success full return of the fox important letters for Lady Franclin at Bagneres Bigorre McClintock.

Sophy helps me upstairs to the privacy of our rooms.

Within the hour, the letters arrive. McClintock's is brief, workmanlike, unembroidered, to the point.

Records discovered at last, two inscriptions scrawled around the margins of a standard Admiralty form buried in a cairn at Victory Point north-west of King William Land.

Sir John Franklin died on the 11th June 1847. *A sadder tale was never told in fewer words*, McClintock states, adding that my husband could not have suffered long and had expired in the hope of success.

I dare not look at Sophy. I have not the words to confide that I have been a widow for twelve years now. I was in Italy when Franklin died – Venice, a crumbling palazzo on the Grand Canal belonging to an exiled duchess friend of mine. At dusk we would retire to the stucco and marble terrace and take a glass of muscatel, watching the sunset, so pretty, so picturesque we said, yet the darkening waters of the lagoon turned blood red. The entire city smelled of pestilence and death. Cholera. June, the worst month.

Strange to think back, I remember Dr King's missive offering his services to search the Great Fish River had arrived that very morning. I should have read it like a portent, instead of screwing the paper in my fist and tossing it to the ground.

Gazing up at my stricken expression, Sophy begins to sob.

'There is nothing to be done,' I say, 'we must not allow our thoughts to run until we return to London.'

Except this evidence proves without doubt that my husband died seven years before Dr John Rae's vile libel. I will not have history defamed by some Hudson Bay trader. Shall seek quiet victory in revenge and demand he be stripped of his reward.

McClintock arrives at dawn before Netty has had time to remove the sheets from the furniture and restore the Japan Room to order, but perhaps it is apt I should receive the good captain surrounded by cobwebs and dust, the gloom of autumnal half light.

McClintock, frailer beyond years since I last saw him. He stoops at the table and busies himself with his papers, setting them out before me. The eager merry countenance Sophy so admired, gone, wiped clean like chalk from a slate.

By his lean palsied frame, I have made an old man of McClintock. All morning, we rake over the facts, second officer Lieutenant Hobson scouring King William's shores north to west, McClintock venturing south.

Master of understatement, my brave commander makes little of the hardships they endured, the swollen legs as if afflicted by dropsy, pains in their joints so excruciating at times they could barely walk – and a man unable to walk could not haul – their gums haemorrhaging blood, signs McClintock recognized as scurvy.

Listening to him describe the ravages of frostbite insidious as a cancer, each stumbling onwards to the repeated cry of how are your feet, stopping at intervals to remove a man's boots, take a good look, rubbing the frozen flesh, I send a silent prayer of thanks. My husband died in the comparative warmth and comfort of his ship. They do not state the cause. But it was unexpected, sudden, perhaps something to do with his heart.

I wonder if he called to me in his final moments – Jane, Jane. How I wish I could have been at his side.

I hope they buried him well. Ransacked the ship for timber, nailed a decent coffin, sewed a fine cambric shroud, lowered him into a narrow plinth of rock hewn by the flicker of a torch with shovels and chisels. If I had listened to Dr King, this nation would have witnessed a state procession, black plumed horses leading the cortège past Buckingham Palace, along the Strand, the streets packed with mourners, weeping, heads bowed. If I had backed Dr King, I would have orchestrated the funeral to perfection. And saved myself twelve senseless years of waiting.

One day, the ice will melt calving great shuddering floes and Franklin's corpse will be recovered, the blue woollen uniform intact, the medals and brass buttons shining bright, even the gold braid of his epaulettes, stiffly tasselled. His solemn face at peace, unbruised, unblemished, as if his life did not seem so far away, as if he had just died.

McClintock is studying me with dark sorrowful eyes. When I look up his gaze flits away from mine. Hard business he's had of it, harbinger of Sir John Franklin's death.

Cold, the teapot stands between us. Neither of us can manage a sip, nor touch the biscuits Netty has arranged on a silver tray.

Patient to the last, I wait for him to continue.

A month into the expedition, Hobson espied an unusual glint through his glass, a strange oblong shape rising from the ridged plains of the north-west coast. He had been deceived before, lured by an ice-blink, Arctic mirage rousing his men into a frenzied race towards the billowing sails of a passing ship only to find a dead gull, wings outstretched, or a gossamer strand of lichen threaded between rocks. The closer he crept, the more fantastical the apparition became, a castle or a medieval keep perched high on precipitous cliffs. Still he persisted until finally he reached a chinked stone cairn standing six feet high. Strewn all around in great piles, blankets, woollens, clothing, four iron boat stoves, kettles and pans neatly stacked as if the travellers intended to return. Adzes, awls, mallets, mattocks, pickaxes, shovels and saws, rope, chain, sailcloth, iron barrel hoops, even brass curtain rods laid out on the snow. It could only be Franklin. Frantically Hobson and his men tore down the cairn and prised the precious note from its sealed brass cylinder. A regular stock form issued to discovery ships with most of the available space occupied by a printed request in six languages that the document should be forwarded to the Secretary of the Admiralty stating the exact time and place at which it was found.

Carefully, I inspect the first inscription penned in bold black ink down one side of the page and perfectly preserved. Even the cheery curlicue flourish of Lieutenant Gore's words – *All well.*

HM Ships Erebus and Terror

28 May 1847, wintered in the ice in

Lat 70° 5' N Long. 98° 23' W

Having wintered in 1846–7 at Beechey Island

in Lat 74° 43' 28" N Long. 91° 39' 15" W

After having ascended Wellington Channel

to Lat 77° and returned by the west side of

Cornwallis Island.

Sir John Franklin commanding the expedition.

All well.

Party consisting of 2 officers and 6 Men left the

ships on Monday 24th May 1847.

McClintock leans over my shoulder.

'An error, Lady Franklin,' he murmurs. 'It was, of course, the winter of 1845–46 they were beset on Beechey Island, which Lieutenant Gore had not thought to correct before signing.'

I force back tears. May, the month my husband was alive.

The second message is harder to decipher, crammed transversely across the margin's rotting blackened edges in Crozier's spidery scrawl.

25 April 1848 – HM Ships Terror and Erebus were deserted on the 22nd April, 5 leagues NNW of this, having been beset since 12 Septr. 1846.

The Officers & Crews consisting of 105 souls – under the command of Captain F.R.M. Crozier landed here – in Lat 69° 37' 42" Long 98° 41' W

Sir John Franklin died on the 11th June 1847 and the total loss by deaths in the Expedition has been to this date 9 officers & 15 men.

He ends:

F.R.M. Crozier

Captain and Senior Officer.

And start tomorrow 26, for Backs Fish River

Also signed by

James Fitzjames

Captain HMS Erebus

I read and check the dates, a mere fortnight between *All Well*, on May 28, 1847, and my husband's death on June 11th. And the following months nine officers and fifteen men died.

Unheard of casualty rate. Some unimaginable calamity must have forced Crozier to abandon his ships on a doomed trek towards Back's Fish River. Is it still possible that several of his party may have survived?

At a loss, I reach out for McClintock's hand.

'Tell me,' I say, 'what do you think might have happened?'

'Have courage, Lady Franklin. Of one thing we are certain.'

From the way this captain looks me straight in the eye, I know he will not desist from the truth.

'Your husband obeyed his instructions. He ventured into Wellington Channel and sailed round Cornwallis Island, a feat none of his rescuers so far have managed.'

Again McClintock studies the scrap of paper.

'If Sir John succeeded in navigating Cornwallis Island, the winter of 1845 must have been extremely mild,' he is saying, 'so mild that it opened the way through Peel Sound allowing him to press onwards to the west of King William Land.'

'West?' I enquire. And all at once, it dawns on me in a sickening flash. My, we have been fools. Duped by the First and Second secretaries of the Admiralty and their dozing clerks commissioned to write up the charts, who fixed that place they call King William Land on Boothia's eastward side.

Diligent and obedient to the last, my husband drove his ships west and readily the floes lured Franklin into their labyrinthine straits then snapped shut on the very threshold of mapped shores. An eastward course would have nudged him into open waters, a stretch of sea to the south and China.

I press my fingers against my temples.

'King William Land does not exist,' I say. 'It is an island. The cartographers were wrong.'

'Have faith, Lady Franklin.' McClintock's voice calm, soothing bristling with masculine authority.

'This record,' he holds up the pitiful remnant, 'proves without doubt Sir John Franklin has been successful in the task the Admiralty set him. He and his men perished for their country and their dearest consolation must have been to know that Englishmen would not rest until they had followed in their footsteps and given to the world what they could not – the grand result of their dreadful journey – the discovery of the North-West Passage.'

With effort, I collect myself. Flatten the tattered corners of the paper, just to touch that first inscription, which my husband might have dictated.

I can hear him still.

No cause for alarm.

Outside, a sharp spatter of rain flung like a fistful of gravel against the pane then lifted by wind once again.

All at once I am struck with the thought, Franklin's death, Jane embodies. Why McClintock's words find me crowned and sceptred by a moral enterprise, which I confess frightens me a little. I alone represent a woman's lot, wife and widow. Not in vain they perished. I must galvanize the public imagination, stir our national reverence for melancholic grandeur, self-sacrifice, the ultimate price of conquest.

What a task I have.

I straighten in my chair.

McClintock gives an encouraging nod.

'There is more, Lady Franklin.'

Hobson trekked southward following the route the survivors might have taken, tracing the barren ice foot some seventy miles, wading thigh deep through melt water pooled by the warming spring.

Many of his men were sick. Some dying. Hobson considered turning back before they suffered the same fate as Crozier's party when one gave a shout.

A shadow on the ice field, a curved timber rib, a stanchion pushing through the snow.

Quickly setting to with shovels, they uncovered a ship's pinnace improbably mounted on a sledge of massive oak beams bound together by iron bolts weighing as much as the cumbersome vessel itself. A sail-rigged boat drawn upon the shore and which by its length and size could only have come from the *Erebus* or the *Terror*.

In the bow, they discovered the skeleton of a tall, well-built, middle-aged man ravaged by wild animals, the mangled bones jumbled among the bare planks. Yet a pair of red and yellow satin slippers edged in black trim remained intact and undisturbed beside a stout pair of leather walking boots.

Another corpse, younger, smaller, wrapped in fox fur, had sought shelter at the stern. Against the boat's side, he had propped two double-barrelled shotguns, muzzle upwards, each loaded and cocked. It is possible he was the last to die. Strewn beneath the after thwarts, cashmere gloves packed with bullets, silk handkerchiefs, towels, ivory combs, sea sponges, soap, toothbrushes, a caddy of loose tea, forty pounds of chocolate still in their foil-wrapped squares, a pouch of tobacco. Silver spoons with my husband's monogram engraved on the handles.

One empty discarded tin, twenty pounds of beef the only provisions.

Books flung about the keel, *A Manual of Private Devotion*, *The Vicar of Wakefield*. Bibles – one underlined in almost every verse, but no journals or messages found.

The boat pointed north-east instead of south towards the Great Fish River.

Evidence that the two men intended to return to the known sanctuary of their vessels.

The pattering squall outside settles into heavy rain, thrumming against the casement, dripping from the sill.

I try to imagine the last survivor, mere boy, his gun primed, ready to fire into the darkness at every sound, every creak in the ice ricocheting in the empty air.

I wonder how long he waited, listened for a footfall, an answering cry, the swift skimming sledges of a passing tribe laden with seal fat. Only the rasp of his breath breaking the silence, the murmured prayers, still alive, alive.

I wonder if he had the courage, could summon the strength to press a loaded muzzle to his temple. Perhaps he would have said the choicest blessing of this life is our power to end it. But his soul flinched from committing a mortal sin. No sense in killing time for time surely would kill him. I wonder. He sleeps, wakes, the shotgun loaded and stationed at his side. Weeps at the prospect of another day, an hour.

McClintock is telling me how he discovered his first skeleton on 25 May of this year, lying prone on a strip of high ground and which from the scraps of his uniform belonged to a steward. Alongside he found a brush, a silver fob watch, a pocket book whose frozen pages revealed nothing when they were thawed and examined beneath a microscope.

Nearby, other corpses were retrieved as if they had fallen and died as they walked.

I shall seal their fates with a widow's grief, my ceaseless tears will immortalize these men.

There's a knock on the door, Netty with a tray.

All day the brave captain and I have been closeted together.

Bowing, McClintock takes his leave.

'Lady Franklin,' he murmurs, raising my hand to his lips. 'Tomorrow the nation will proclaim you now hold the highest position of any English woman.'

I look up and smile. It is exhausting work. It will take years to be done. There will be quibbles of course. Certain rules need to be changed, particularly since the expedition failed to return with news of its triumph alive.

I anticipate the usual opposition, John Rae, Robert McClure and their dissenters, brandishing reward certificates, knighthoods of course.

It will cost me my strength. There will be no rest but I will prevail summoning my assault troops, experienced credible men, Richardson, Grinnell, McClintock,

Osborn, Collinson. I will use every influence in the land until the name of the Discoverer of the North-West Passage is forever linked to that of my husband, Sir John Franklin.

And just when I have claimed victory – perhaps a Founder's Gold Medal from the Royal Geographical Society – dangled in my palm, the first woman ever so honoured, there will be the matter of the monument to attend presiding on endless committees elected by government.

That plinth in Trafalgar Square will be Franklin's.

McClintock has gone. Too weary now to discuss the day's events with Sophy.

Netty tiptoes about the room, clears away the untouched supper on the table. I ask her not to draw the curtains. For hours I recline on the divan and gaze out at the wheeling constellations, the favourites from my childhood, the Bear, the Plough, that arching giant, Orion straddling the heavens, the silver points of his belt, the scimitar glint of his sword veiled with clouds.

I am tempted to open the window wide. Lean out and inhale the night scents, wood smoke, the brine tang of mists unfurling from the Thames, wreathed across the mud flats like ghosts from the dead.

I think of my husband, posing for his daguerreotype, unsmiling and stern and Crozier behind him waiting his turn. I think of Fitzjames, De Voeux, Fairholm, fine, handsome boys. But mostly my thoughts return to that youth, forsaken and alone in the stern of a boat endlessly adrift across fields of ice, firing his gun, the shots blasting indigo skies, those shimmering familiars, the Bear, the Plough.

I shiver. Tomorrow, my life's work lies ahead. Time for a cup of hot milk laced with cinnamon and rum. Time for bed.

I ring the bell for Netty.

Epilogue

In 1865, the American arctic adventurer Charles Francis Hall encountered a group of Eskimos (Inuit) who stated that an officer and another white man had last been seen alive in 1858 trekking across the Barrens. These survivors from the Franklin expedition indicated they were returning home. Later still gunshots could be heard across the ice.

Jane Franklin triumphed in her campaign to exalt her husband as the man who forged the last link with his life.

In 1866, a statue of Franklin was erected in London's Waterloo Place with the inscription proclaiming that he and his companions sacrificed their lives in completing the discovery of the North-West Passage. A replica of the statue was sent to Hobart, Tasmania where it still stands in Franklin Square.

A memorial was held in Westminster Abbey in

July 1875. The epitaph composed by the Poet Laureate Alfred Tennyson reads:

> *Not here: The white North hath thy bones and thou,*
> *Heroic Sailor Soul*
> *Art passing on thy happier voyage now*
> *Towards no earthly pole.*

Jane died at the age of eighty-three on 18 July 1875, two weeks before the unveiling ceremony.

After Jane Franklin's death, Sophy Cracoft devoted the rest of her life to collating her aunt's correspondence and diaries comprising two thousand letters and two hundred journals. She went blind before completing the massive task and died on 20 June 1892 aged seventy-seven. She never married.

Eleanor and John Gell reconciled with Jane Franklin, who offered them a generous percentage of her property investments in Tasmania and received the young couple at her home. Sophy, who would never forgive Eleanor, wrote: 'Kind of course was my Aunt's reception of them – warmer than their greeting or demeanour.'

John Rae received the ten thousand pound Admiralty reward but was publicly discredited for his allegations about the Franklin expedition and refused a knighthood.

Acknowledgements

All my thanks to my publisher Charlotte (Charlie) Greig for her encouragement, insights and critical judgement, Nicholas Blake for his meticulous efforts in putting me right on historical and maritime matters and the entire team at Picador UK.

I also thank the Literature Board of the Australia Council for the generous grant which allowed me to complete this work.

For my primary source in researching *Fields of Ice*, I relied heavily on *Portrait of Jane, A Life of Lady Franklin* by Francis J. Woodward, Hodder & Stoughton, 1951.

I am also indebted to the following inspiring works of scholarship: *Sir John Franklin and the Arctic Regions* by P. L. Simmonds, Nonsuch Publishing, 1852; *The Search for Franklin* by Leslie H. Neatby, Arthur Baker Limited, 1970; *Frozen in Time* by Owen Beattie and John Greiger, Grafton Books, 1987; *Arctic Dreams* by Barry Lopez,

Scribner's Sons, 1986; *Barrow's Boys* by Fergus Fleming, Granta Books, 1998; *I May Be Some Time, Ice and the English Imagination* by Francis Spufford, Faber & Faber, 1997; *Ice Blink* by Scott Cookman, John Wiley & Sons, 2000; *Deadly Winter* by Martyn Beardsley, Chatham Publishing, 2002; *Steering to Glory, A Day in the Life of a Ship of the Line* by Nicholas Blake, Chatham Publishing, 2005; *Lady Franklin's Revenge* by Ken McGoogan, Bantam Press, 2006; *Captain Francis Crozier, Last Man Standing* by Michael Smith, the Collins Press, 2006.